The Chinese Knot

and other stories

LIEN CHAO

We acknowledge the support of the Canada Council for the Arts for our publishing
program and the Government of Ontario through the Ontario Arts Council.

 Canada Council for the Arts   Conseil des Arts du Canada   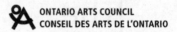 ONTARIO ARTS COUNCIL CONSEIL DES ARTS DE L'ONTARIO

Cover design by Heng Wee Tan

"Neighbours" was first published in *Strike the Wok: An Anthology of Chinese Canadian Fiction* (2003) Chao, Lien and Wong-Chu, Jim, eds. (TSAR Publications).

Library and Archives Canada Cataloguing in Publication

Chao, Lien, 1950–
 The Chinese knot and other stories / Lien Chao.

Short stories.
ISBN 978-1-894770-43-9

I. Title.

PS8555.H3955C44 2008   C813'.54   C2007-907675-0

Printed in Canada by Coach House Printing

TSAR Publications
P. O. Box 6996, Station A
Toronto, Ontario M5W 1X7
Canada

www.tsarbooks.com

I dedicate this book to Peng Ma who believes in art

Contents

Introduction

SINCE THE EARLY 1980s, a large number of Chinese immigrants have settled in Toronto, my family among them. Two decades later, 43% of Torontonians reported themselves as belonging to a visible minority group, the Chinese being the largest community.[1] Interested in finding out how the Chinese immigrants have fared in Toronto, I took my mental camera, so to speak, to the city's busy streets to catch snapshots of their lives. I have been to Chinatown, ESL classes, community centres, university campuses, private homes, public libraries, coffee shops, restaurants, art galleries, the City Hall, and Yonge Street. The stories collected here have emerged from these inner-city snapshots. The characters, based on real-life models, have been given fictitious names and are, except for a few friends, mostly strangers. But all of them are single Chinese women, because it is their lives that interested me most.

These precious friends and strangers, over the last twenty-odd years, have narrated to me how their lives and relationships have altered after immigration, and gradually how they themselves have changed to become part of the Canadian scene. Their stories touched me unforgettably.

Immigrants go through a continuous cultural processing to become Canadian. What happens in every corner of our cities every day are stories of their adaptation, willing or otherwise, to a new language, different customs, employment in a new country, and changes in personal and family relationships. Such processes generate emotional conflicts in all of us, as we struggle to keep some part of ourselves intact; at the same time, the inevitable adaptation gives us a sense of growth and accomplishment. Through racial and cultural interactions, mutual understanding among citizens is stimulated. As Canadians we optimistically believe that together we are weaving the tapestry of a better society, more intense in colour and complex in texture.

I thank my publishers for asking Jim Wong-Chu and myself to edit a collection of contemporary Chinese Canadian short fiction in 2003, entitled *Strike the Wok*, from which my desire to write short stories began. I also want to express my heartfelt gratitude to my dear friend Virginia Rock who was the first reader of these stories; her encouragement and support have always been indispensable. I thank the Ontario Arts Council Writers' Reserve Program for its timely support of the project. And above all, I thank all my friends and acquaintances and all the strangers I have met in this city for their precious stories.

[1] http://www.toronto.ca/toronto_facts/diversity.htm

Under the Monkey Bars

SWINGING HER ARMS, Wei Ming takes large strides across Monarch Park towards the kids' playground. The fenced enclosure at the southwestern corner of the park has been in her peripheral vision for nearly a decade. Today, for the first time since she moved into this East-end neighbourhood, the gated playground is the center of her attention. She walks on the grass alongside the fence, wondering how to get inside. A patch of orange paint on the black metal fence calls her attention to a latch. She lifts up the bar and steps in gingerly, like a kid going to the daycare for the first time. Closing the gate behind her, she hears the bar fall back with a clang. Young parents throw suspicious glances at her as if to inquire why she has come without the company of a child.

There are two slides in the playground. The bigger one is made of wood, the smaller one of metal. Another structure with a dozen yellow metal tubes is bent into a U-shape and fastened onto two long bars parallel to each other and about two feet apart. Wei Ming thinks this equipment must be the monkey bars and she walks towards it. She looks up at it like a child, stretches her arms, and stands up on her tiptoes to reach a bar; as soon as her hands touch it, a sharp pain shoots through her spine.

"Ouch!" She lets go of the bar.

Catching her breath, she inhales deeply before stretching up her arms again. This time she manages to put her hands on the bar above her head. Holding her breath tightly, she counts silently, one—two—three—four—five, before letting it out slowly. Her whole mind attends to the trembling pain shooting down from her left shoulder. She grins, takes in another deep breath, holds it tightly like a balloon, and counts one to five again before exhaling.

It is a beautiful afternoon. Maples and oaks are draped in radiant fall colours. Dog owners have gathered on the slope east of the playground. While the animals chase and yelp at each other, their owners casually exchange gossip. Their conversations usually start from the subject of their dogs and then move on to the neighbourhood. They tell each other the latest real estate news, who has sold their house for how much, and how the new neighbours are an immigrant family from Asia, and so on. From time to time one of them pitches a baseball or a frisbee, interrupting the conversation. The nervy dogs immediately rush out towards the projectiles while the lazy ones only bark and wag their tails excitedly.

Inside the fenced playground, two kids go up and down on a teeter-totter; another one is on a swing, and two more are on the big slide. Three parents stand by, talking to each other and watching their children. Wei Ming inhales deeply, her hands tight on the monkey bar. She closes her eyes to concentrate on her shoulder. Where does the pain come from—from her muscle, tendon, or ligament? She isn't sure; she only knows it is a problem that has increasingly preoccupied her mind. It all started a few months back when she couldn't bend her left arm to clasp her bra at the back. Since then she has changed her habit to fastening her bra at the front and then rotating it to the back.

"You've got what the Chinese call 'fifty-year-old shoulder,'" her friend Rose said. "Or frozen shoulder, as a western doctor would say. Are you fifty yet?"

"What kind of logic is that? Does that mean everybody will get it upon reaching fifty?" Wei Ming is fifty-two this year.

"Sounds fair, doesn't it? The good thing is that you don't really have to do anything about it. Eventually the pain will go away. So cheer up." Rose laughed.

Waiting with hope and disbelief for the pain to go away, Wei Ming tried not to use her left arm. But when she couldn't reach her eyebrows or comb her hair with her left hand any more, she despaired. She went to see Dr Simons, her family doctor, who sent her for an X-ray. She also went to see a sports physician, who sent her for an ultrasound. Before another specialist sent her for a CT, or whatever, and eventually to a surgeon as Dr Simons had already suggested to her, she started looking for alternative medicine practitioners in the local Chinese papers. She browsed through a huge list of herbalists, acupuncturists, and registered massage therapists. A Dr Lin with the credential of "a former Chinese Olympic Teams' medical doctor" caught her attention.

While Dr Simons advised Wei Ming to stop using her left arm in the habitual way to avoid further damage, Dr Lin gave her a different and typically Chinese philosophy upon her first visit. "Don't let pain control you. You take control of the pain. Work into the pain."

With her hands on the monkey bars and her feet on the sandy ground, Wei Ming repeats the sequence of inhaling, holding, and exhaling. She can hear leaves rustle on the branches in the warm afternoon breeze as she performs her stretching exercises. They are changing colours as she is counting her seconds on the monkey bars. How delicate life is. She remembers a recent *Toronto Star* article, in which a columnist wrote that there are one hundred and fifty-four colours between red and green in the Canadian autumn. But the writer didn't say how he counted the colours and hues. Right now, surrounded by all these colours, Wei Ming feels exuberantly peaceful, even her shoulder pain feels alleviated.

"Xiao Bao, go to the small slide," a man's voice speaks in Wei Ming's mother tongue. Hearing people speaking Chinese or other Asian languages in this mixed neighbourhood is no longer a surprise to anyone. In Toronto, most Chinese speak Cantonese or Mandarin; Wei Ming is surprised that this man speaks the Henan dialect. She recalls that historically Henan was a poor, underdeveloped province in China and its people were laughed at when they travelled to big cities like Shanghai and Beijing. They were stereotyped as country bumpkins for their lack of manners and style. Wei Ming opens her eyes to see a man in his early thirties: a buzz haircut, a pair of rimless glasses, and a white polo shirt of the latest fashion. He is seated on a bench, waving at a boy of three or four years of age who stands at the foot of the slide watching other kids.

"Go to the small slide, Xiao Bao!" The young father raises his voice at the boy and points at the smaller slide on the other side of the playground.

"No, no, I want to play with them!" Xiao Bao talks back at his father, showing a trait of stubbornness, if not an early rebellion. He also speaks the Henan dialect and sounds quite charming to Wei Ming's ear.

"Now listen to me, Xiao Bao, before you get hurt, go to the small slide over there!" the father insists.

Wei Ming has seen enough young Chinese parents take exceeding care in the supervision of their children; like Xiao Bao's father, they sometimes spoil their fun and aggravate the onlooker.

"They are going to hurt you, the big boys." Suddenly the father raises his voice to a high pitch, "Watch out! A *Xiao Hei* and *Ah Cha* are . . . !" Before he finishes his sentence, he dashes out from the bench. Like a twister he grabs his son with tremendous energy and jumps at least a meter away from the slide as if to avoid a collision.

Who is *Xiao Hei*? And *Ah Cha*? Wei Ming is puzzled. The two boys coming down the slide are not even Chinese. Why did Xiao Bao's father refer to them by these ridiculous Chinese names?

A sharp pain cuts through Wei's nerves. Her hands drop down from the monkey bars. It has just dawned on her that the young father, who treasures his own son as Xiao Bao, Little Precious, refers to the other boys by derogatory Chinese nicknames. *Xiao Hei* means

"Little Black," describing skin colour, but Wei Ming has no idea what *Ah Cha* means except for its totally disparaging racial connotation. Now that the two boys have landed on the ground noisily, Wei Ming notices that one boy is Black and the other South Asian.

Wei Ming's face turns red and her ears burn. Looking around the playground, she sees the puzzled expressions on other parents' faces. She realizes that besides Xiao Bao and his father, she is the only other Chinese on the playground who understands what is going on and has been said. She is ashamed of herself for witnessing such an episode in the kids' playground, feeling like a conspirator with the father and son. Before someone else notices her embarrassment, Wei Ming decides to end her exercises.

The latch on the gate clangs heavily behind her as she quickly steps out of the playground.

In the morning when Wei Ming comes to the park, it is a different scene. Vapoury air surrounds the tree trunks and morning dew rolls on the fallen leaves, dampening the sandy ground underneath the monkey bars. Squirrels are running up and down the tree trunks; sparrows are darting in and out of the branches. Inside the playground, Wei Ming sees prints of curved-in nails in the sand and wonders what kind of animal was here at night. There are no kids at this time of the day and it is almost too quiet for a public park except for birds chirping away, and every ten minutes the clanking of wheels as the Go Train passes by on the south side of the park. Wei Ming fills her lungs with cool, fresh air; she stretches her arms upwards to rest her hands on the last yellow bar; holding her breath, she bends her knees a little at a time, gradually giving her body in to gravity and losing herself to the sight of the trees surrounding the playground. As she swings her arms gently she can see the rising sun torch the upper part of the trees, giving them a warm glow. She lets out a deep breath, imagining herself at a campsite surrounded by a lot more trees and birds.

"Zao Sang! Zao Sang!" A group of elderly Chinese men gather under a huge maple tree on the north side of the playground. They speak Cantonese, a southern Chinese dialect, totally different from Mandarin. Wei Ming doesn't understand Cantonese, so she has no idea what they are talking about at the top of their lungs. She can see that the elders have already put on their down-padded winter over-coats, grey or black in colour, as if it were a minus twenty deep-freeze in winter. With the hoods on and tied down under their chins, their faces appear smaller and indistinguishable from one another. Wei Ming hopes to see the elders do Taichi or some other Chinese martial art exercises, but they just stand there in a small circle, hands in their coat pockets, talking passionately among themselves. Do psychologists say men are less talkative? These old Chinese men certainly have a lot to say to each other. Maybe they don't have anyone to talk to at home; maybe they live in the seniors' residences by themselves. Coming to the park and talking to their peers may well be the only conversation they have in a day.

"Zao Sang! Zao Sang!" A group of Cantonese-speaking elderly Chinese women enter the park from the southwestern side, probably through the Go Train railroad tunnel. Wei Ming thinks the women probably know the men and will likely join them under the maple tree to form a bigger circle of gossipers. But to her surprise, the women take their walk on the west side of the park. They stop under a willow to swing their arms. Maybe they also suffer from "fifty-year-old shoulders," Wei Ming thinks, although they seem to be much older than fifty. Perhaps she should tell them to come and hang from the monkey bars. That would make a scene, wouldn't it! Wei Ming smiles, imagines half a dozen old Chinese women hanging from the monkey bars. After swinging their arms for a few minutes, they walk further away. Wei Ming watches them merge into the brilliant fall colours, blending in with the glistening frail leaves in the bright morning sunshine.

"Zao Sang! Zao Sang!" Wei Ming greets the elderly men on her way out of the park after finishing her exercises. The men look quite astonished. But as soon as they start speaking to her, they are disappointed to find out that she only knows two words of their language.

So she is just like the *Queilao*, a white ghost, a Caucasian, who sometimes can even say four words in Cantonese, such as *Kung Hei Fat Choi* during the Chinese New Year.

Wei Ming wishes she could speak Cantonese, but for their own sakes she wishes the elderly Chinese men could speak some English. She has heard that many *Lao Hua Qiao*, "old overseas Chinese," have managed to live in Canada for thirty or forty years without speaking English. She has read the reason why, which is that in the past the Canadian labour market had discriminated against the Chinese, who thus ended up working in Chinatown. But there is another reason that she now begins to see—the Chinese elders don't feel comfortable mingling with people other than their own kind. What she has observed from under the monkey bars is that if the Chinese elders really want to break through their isolation, they can definitely do it today. In this mixed neighbourhood, they only need to get a dog, and then they could join the dog owners on the slope, who talk in English. Maybe they could bring a grandchild to the playground; they would soon be chatting with other parents and grandparents in English. Or if they had the courage to lift up the latch on the metal fence, they could even walk inside the playground and swing on the monkey bars.

Who says it doesn't take nerve to walk into a kids' playground without a child in tow? It has been two weeks since Wei Ming started stretching on the monkey bars, but none of the parents have spoken to her yet. They simply ignore her and she can see why. Although she doesn't look too old to be the mother of a toddler, without one she doesn't fit into the parent-children group. Just as without a dog it would be awkward for her to walk over to the slope and stand among the dog owners. But Wei Ming still thinks the young parents have been quite tolerant with her intrusion. They can stop her from using the monkey bars anytime simply by collecting enough signatures and having the city post a sign saying "For Children Only" in the playground.

Wei Ming's neighbours at the townhouse complex have done a

similarly nasty thing to another neighbour. Shortly after they had moved into their new townhouse, the Chinese family next door put a basketball hoop above their garage. In the late afternoon and early evening, Wei Ming could hear kids from the elementary and junior high schools playing basketball in the back lane. Sometimes she would stand on the back porch watching them like a cheerleader. But a childless couple living at the head of the block agitated against the kids. Two weeks later signs appeared everywhere in the back lanes, "Ball and Hockey Playing Prohibited." That afternoon when a city bylaw officer came to the compound, Wei Ming was home, but none of the signing neighbours showed their faces. As she opened the sliding door of her kitchen, she heard the officer express his sympathy to the kids. "I grew up playing street hockey myself. So, just to let you and your parents know that if you can collect more signatures than they did, you could apply to have these signs removed."

But the neighbours didn't collect signatures from sympathizers like Wei Ming. She had waited for them a few evenings and was disappointed that they didn't put up a fight. But why didn't they take down the basketball hoop? It has been hanging there above their garage for nearly a decade now, watching over the neighbourhood like a lone sentry. During this time the kids have grown up; one by one they have left home for universities. Now the oldest son is a parent himself. Sometimes he returns home to visit his parents over the weekends. Wei Ming imagines him looking at the hoop perched above the back lanes, and the bullying signs that managed to destroy his childhood fun. Even today he cannot shoot a few sentimental balls before dinner without breaking the city bylaw.

How do they feel about this? What will the young father tell his son when his toddler grows up and wants to play basketball at his grandparents' house? How does the cantankerous childless couple feel about destroying the kids' fun? Wei Ming wonders sometimes. From the day the signs were put up, she has stopped talking to them. The neighbours who put up the basketball hoop have done the same. Year after year they watch the other couple renovate their back porch with its fancy garden, its tall evergreens in big clay flower pots and dead trees replaced by new ones each spring. Climbing vines have woven the deck fence with large foliage so that during the summer and fall the two people, joined sometimes by their friends, can enjoy a barbecue and sunbathe on the deck half naked as if no neighbours can see them.

In late October after Thanksgiving, the days are getting shorter and few leaves are left still hanging on the branches. Leaves fallen under the trees feel like a thick carpet. Wei Ming's shoulder is much better now; not only can she bend her knees easily under the monkey bar, she can also swing her body back and forth while standing on tiptoes. Since she doesn't have to grit her teeth or close her eyes to work into her pain any more when hanging and stretching her arms, she has time to watch other people on the playground. She notices a little girl, three or four years old, looking up at her curiously through a pair of glasses; her chubby little hands rest on a spinning barrel installed onto the side of the large slide, her big blue eyes clear like water.

"What's your name?" Wei Ming asks the little one.

"Vivienne," she smiles, and a dimple appears on each of her chubby cheeks.

"That's a lovely name," Wei Ming says. "How old are you, Vivienne?"

"Three years and two months," the little girl answers seriously.

"Do you have back problems?" Vivienne's mother asks Wei Ming.

"Shoulder, frozen shoulder. But it's a lot better now," Wei Ming answers positively. She doesn't like to talk about her problems with strangers.

"That's good, we've seen you work hard on the monkey bars." The woman smiles warmly.

Wei Ming doesn't remember seeing Vivienne and her mother before. "I must have been totally absorbed in my own problems," she mumbles to herself.

A black girl of about five or six is standing on top of the large slide. "Let me show you how to work on the monkey bars," she says and climbs over the railings to get over to the bars from above. Over on this side now, she hangs on the first bar with both hands and starts to swing her body. With a strong forward motion, she quickly grabs onto the next bar with one hand; her legs kicking in the air, she continues to swing her body forward and grabs the next bar ahead with her other hand. She moves so fast on the bars one after another that Wei Ming has to get out of her way quickly in order to let her reach the last bar.

"This is—how—you do—it," the girl jumps down and lands on both feet, having reached the last bar. Breathlessly, she says, "I just want to—show—you." Tiny beads of sweat shine on the tip of her nose. "My name—is—Stella." She stretches out a hand towards Wei Ming. "What's—your name?"

Wei Ming is totally taken aback by the friendly gesture. For more than two weeks she has been quietly hanging on the last monkey bar twice a day, each time for about twenty minutes. She has hardly talked to anyone except delivering her daily "Zao Sang" to the Cantonese-speaking seniors under the big maple. She has no idea how the kids' world functions here, let alone how to make friends with them. As far as she can tell, the parents control the playground and who their children are allowed to play with; at least that was her memory of a kids' playground before she entered this one.

Twenty-some years ago, when her daughter was five Wei Ming got divorced. In the early eighties divorce was rare and seen to be as tragic as a premature death. A few friends expressed their sympathy to her, but most people she knew, including colleagues and neighbours, blamed her for being an outspoken woman, using an old Chinese expression which says that a husband beating his wife is like teeth biting the tongue—often happens and nothing to be alarmed about. In her neighbourhood, people talked behind her back, while children nicknamed Wei Ming's daughter "the fatherless," and refused to play with her.

Now standing in front of Wei Ming, this lovely girl, as old as her daughter was when she divorced, is looking at her earnestly, wanting to make her acquaintance. Clumsily, Wei Ming stretches out her right hand and stammers, "Oh, Stella, it's nice meeting you, my name is Wei Ming. And thank you for showing me how to work the monkey bars." She doesn't know how to express her excitement at being offered friendship by someone so young in front of her peers and their parents.

"Hi, Wei Ming!" Stella shakes Wei Ming's hand.

"Hello, Wei Ming! Wei Ming, I am Adam!" A boy on the swing throws over a greeting.

"That's my brother, Adam," Stella introduces. "He will be five-years-old on Christmas Day."

Almost instantly, Wei Ming recalls having seen Adam's face before. He was the boy at the top of the large slide when the Chinese boy Xiao Bao was at the bottom before being taken away by his father.

"Now, do you know how to work the monkey bars, Wei Ming?" Stella draws Wei Ming's attention.

Wei Ming smiles, wondering whether Stella will now act as if she were her coach. She nods enthusiastically. "I think so, Stella, thank you very much." She just can't believe that Stella and the other kids treat her as an equal on the playground rather than as another adult on-looker.

"Want to give it another try?" Stella continues to direct Wei Ming.

"OK, this time I will try to lift my feet off the ground." Lifting up both her feet at the same time has been her goal ever since she started exercising on the monkey bars. Taking her gloves off and gripping tightly, she moves her hands around to find the best spot. Then with both arms straight above her, she takes in a deep breath, holding it in tightly, and slowly lets go of the ground under her feet. For the next one or two short seconds, Wei Ming knows she has made her biggest progress. "I have done it! I have done it! Stella! I actually did it!" She cries out loudly.

"You did?" Stella looks at Wei Ming suspiciously.

"Yes, I did, I have lifted my feet off the ground!"

No one has any idea how much pain she has endured in the past two weeks in order to do this today, but it doesn't matter any more because she has conquered her pain. Looking into Stella's expectant eyes, Wei Ming teases the girl, "Maybe by next spring, when I grow up a bit more, I'll be able to do what you did today."

A mischievous smile appears on the girl's face. "Yeah? OK!"

"Stella! Come over, please!" Adam, on the swing, is calling his sister. Stella runs over to help her brother come down. The boy walks straight to the sand pit, where Vivienne's mother is showing the kids how to make sand cupcakes with a plastic mold. Vivienne and Xiao Bao are sitting inside the pit, each with a plastic cup to scoop up the sand. Xiao Bao's father is sitting on the bench reading a thick computer manual.

"*Xiao Hei! Xiao Hei!*" Xiao Bao stands up and yells at Adam in his Henan dialect.

The young father frowns and raises his eyebrows a little from the book. "OK, OK, never mind the devil," he mumbles and continues his reading.

A surge of disagreeable feeling overcomes Wei Ming, submerging her happiness under mucky water—her fresh, innocent friendship with the kids and their parents in the golden autumn sunshine has suddenly vanished. She recalls the time when she overheard Xiao Bao's father call Adam and the South Asian boy by derogatory Chinese nicknames, when she simply walked out of the playground without a word of protest. Today, after meeting Vivienne and her mother, and then Stella and Adam, she feels she can no longer walk away silently from such a scene.

"Take control of the pain." Dr Lin's words ring in her ears again as she stretches her arms upwards.

Wei Ming also remembers a famous Canadian woman she met recently at a community event, whose first name is June, like the month in summer. June asked the crowd what they would do if they happened to see an injustice on the street. As the crowd responded variously, June said that each person had an obligation to do something, otherwise you were no longer a spectator, you had become a participant in the injustice.

Wei Ming walks slowly towards the sand pit, wondering how June would handle the situation if she were here.

Inside the sand pit, Vivienne's mother is offering plastic cups to Stella and Adam. "Want to join us make some cupcakes?" she invites the brother and sister.

"We know how to make a sand castle," says Stella proudly.

"Really, Stella? Why don't you show us how to make a sand castle?" Vivienne's mother stands up to give Stella her place.

"Stella," Wei Ming interrupts, standing beside the sand pit. "What's your brother's name?"

"His name is Adam," the sister answers loudly, clearing up the sand pit.

"Adam, what a proud name," Wei Ming exclaims, clapping her hands.

Vivienne's mother echoes, "Yes, it is. Adam is a great Christian name."

"Adam, do you want to tell Xiao Bao your name?" Wei Ming pats Adam's shoulders softly.

"Sure, Xiao Bao, want to know my name? My name is Adam," he says to the Chinese boy.

"Adam? OK! Adam!" Standing up from the sand pit, Xiao Bao runs towards the bench where his father is sitting. "Daddy—Daddy, his name is Adam, it is Adam, not *Xiao Hei*," the boy shouts in English.

The young father lifts his eyes from the book. Leaning back on the bench, his look sweeping across the playground, he grabs his son's small shoulders with both hands. "Adam, so it's Adam . . ." He repeats the name as if to savour its quality before he stretches his back and looks afar at the western horizon, now covered with the crimson clouds of autumn.

The sun is setting. Xiao Bao's father stands up from the bench, inhales deeply, holding in the breath, and then, quietly, he exhales. As his chest heaves up and down, Wei Ming can see his glasses mirror the blazing clouds and colourful leaves.

Rose

"WHAT DO YOU CALL HER?" Rose asks Alice, who is twelve. Alice throws a quick glance at her mother Qing walking beside her.

"So what do you call her, Alice?" Rose repeats her question loudly, pointing a finger at Qing.

This time it is Qing who makes anxious eye contact with Alice, assuring her daughter that her friend Rose is truly not herself today. There are other pedestrians on the sidewalk. Qing suspects they must have heard Rose as well because she asked the question in English.

It has been seven or eight years since Qing last saw Rose. Bumping into her like this on Bloor Street in downtown Toronto is a great surprise. But before they have had a chance to exchange a greeting, why does Rose ask Alice such a ridiculous question?

"I—call—my—mother—Mum." Alice spits out her words one by one with emphasis.

"So you call her Mum, ah?" Rose echoes.

Qing looks at Rose helplessly, wondering what she is going to say next.

"Of course you call her Mum, because she is your mother. And you should call her Mum! You should, but . . ." Rose hesitates. A young couple waiting at the intersection throws over a curious glance at her.

Rose looks around at other pedestrians on the sidewalks. "My

15

daughter refuses to address me, she doesn't call me Mum or Mummy, as if I am not her mother at all!" Suddenly her voice becomes tearful.

"That's terrible," a young woman utters. "Why is she like that? How old is your daughter?"

"Twelve years old, just like Alice." Rose nods towards Alice. Qing wishes she could talk to her friend in private, at least not on one of Toronto's busiest streets.

"Where are you going, Rose?" Qing asks, recalling that her friend lives in Scarborough in the east end of the city.

"I am staying with my friend Kim at Dupont and St George."

"Oh . . ."

Now Qing senses something must have gone quite wrong for Rose, otherwise she wouldn't be staying at a friend's. Rose's short hair is completely grey. Anxiety has carved many fine lines around her eyes and across her forehead. Her glasses are foggy with dust. In dim twilight, Rose looks pale and fragile with a few age spots on her cheeks. "Would you like to come for dinner tomorrow?" Qing invites.

It must have been a decade ago, Qing remembers, at a party organized by the International Students' Centre at the University of Toronto, when she first met Rose, a scientist who tested air quality in the city. To Qing and other Chinese visa students at that time, Rose was a great success. She was one of the few scholars from Mainland China who actually had a real job and earned a decent salary.

"When I was interviewed for the job," Rose told a crowd of overseas Chinese students at the party who were anxious to learn about her success story, "my boss said that this job was as stable as an 'Iron Rice Bowl.' But it was for someone who wouldn't mind doing the most tedious and repetitive work in the entire lab. Previous technicians hired for this position got bored so quickly that they left the lab one after another within the first year. So this time, the boss made it clear to the candidates that he was looking for someone who wouldn't leave. So what do you think I told him?" Rose paused to ask the enthusiastic listeners.

"You promised him you wouldn't leave," the crowd answered altogether.

"Exactly. I told him I love doing the basic tests and wouldn't mind doing them three times a day. And if I got the job, I would keep it until my retirement. The boss hired me on the spot." Rose smiled at the crowd.

However, three years later, Rose lost her "Iron Rice Bowl" due to the provincial government's education funding cut. By then, she had sponsored her husband and daughter to come over from China and they were renting a two-bedroom apartment on Huron Street near Chinatown.

One afternoon, Qing was shopping in Chinatown when she saw a middle-aged woman try to load a four-drawer dresser onto a supermarket shopping cart. Her awkwardness made quite a scene on the sidewalk. Qing stepped forward to help, and saw that the woman was actually Rose.

"Hey, what are you doing here, Rose?"

"Oh, Qing, it's you." Rose was out of breath and somewhat embarrassed. "I found this dresser. Someone has thrown it out, but I can use it at home."

"Yeah, why not, it's a good dresser, it's even hardwood." Qing helped Rose stabilize the furniture on top of the shopping cart. "How's your daughter? And your husband?"

"Ugh, don't mention him. He wouldn't lend a finger even if the dresser were right outside our house," Rose said resentfully.

"Has he been looking for work since he came to Canada?"

"He's had two jobs. The first one was a manager's position at a luggage store, but he quit in the second month because he couldn't stand the boss's wife giving him orders. The second was a salesman's job at a shoe store. This time he couldn't put up with the boss's daughter fussing around the store, and he left the job in the first week. After that, he hasn't even had one job interview."

"That's too bad, he doesn't seem to understand that Canada is a capitalist country and most of the businesses are private, especially the service industry. An employee has to get along with the employer's entire family in order to keep the job," Qing said sympathetically.

"That's what I said to him. Like you, I felt sorry for him at the beginning, because he is not familiar with the Canadian system. But one day I heard that a friend's friend, who owns a gift store, was looking for a manager. So I asked my husband for his resumé. Guess what I found out?" The two women stopped on the sidewalk to catch their breath. Rose waited for Qing to make a guess.

Qing did a quick search in her mind, but she had no clue. So she said boldly, "He anglicized his name?"

"Ugh, ugh." Rose shook her head.

"He forged a certificate of some Canadian qualification?"

"That would be a logical thing to do, wouldn't it?" Rose laughed sarcastically.

Qing scratched her head, "Then I have no idea how innovative he can be."

"My husband is an original. You are not going to believe this—no one would! In his resumé, under the category of work experience, he wrote, 'Party Secretary for the Canton Import and Export Bureau for fifteen years.'" Rose paused, waiting for Qing to respond.

Stunned, Qing burst out, "Oh, my God! I can't believe this! Is this guy out of his mind? Did he think he would impress employers with his Party credentials? He must be totally mad to believe a Canadian employer would hire a Chinese Communist Party boss to sit in the company office." Qing went on, "I'm sorry, Rose. I am shocked by his honesty."

"Honesty?" Rose raised her voice, "Honesty has nothing to do with stupidity, does it? But later I realized why he did this; it's because he simply doesn't want to work. You see, he speaks good English plus Mandarin and Cantonese, he has twenty years' work experience in import and export business; he should be able to find some work to do when so many Canadian companies want to do business in China. When he told me he had faxed his resumé to hundreds of businesses,

I was puzzled why there was not even a single job interview."

"But this is suicidal, why did he do this?" Qing asked.

"No idea." Rose shook her head sadly.

"So has he been able to make some other contributions to the family?"

"Ugh, ugh, none, whatsoever. And he says that since I have sponsored him to come to Canada, according to law I am responsible for supporting him for four years, until he receives his Canadian passport. After that he will go to Hong Kong to make money."

"Sounds like he is totally irresponsible. Maybe he didn't want to come to Canada."

"Yes, he did," Rose corrected Qing 's assumption immediately. "He dreamt of coming to Canada for many years. I'll tell you about his strategic immigration plan some other time."

The two women pushed the dresser to a semidetached, two-storey house on Huron Street where Rose and her family were renting at the time.

When the doorbell rings, Qing is in the kitchen, chopping mushrooms, green peppers, and yellow onions, preparing to make spaghetti for dinner.

"Are you crying for me?" Rose grins at the doorway.

"Yeah, want to join me?" She dabs her eyes, wet from cutting onions, with a tissue. Rose wears a summer dress, a gold necklace and a pair of dangling earrings. If she would just dye her hair, Qing thinks, her friend would look ten years younger.

In the kitchen, Rose takes over. She starts to sauté the onions and garlic with ground beef. Then she throws in hot pepper, green pepper, mushroom, Italian herbs, and pours in a tall can of tomato sauce. Her dexterity with different cooking utensils suggests that a professional chef is in the kitchen, and soon the sauce is simmering under the glass lid of the wok. Qing watches her friend with open admiration.

"Hey, Rose, you look like a master of the kitchen."

"You probably didn't know I was a housekeeper in New York for three years before immigrating to Canada," Rose says, stirring the sauce.

"You never told me," replies Qing. "I thought you came as an environmental scientist."

"That's later. I came to Canada as a housekeeper because I worked as one for an Italian family in Manhattan. They were a very nice young couple with two boys. And I learned to cook Italian food—angel hair, fettuccini, jumbo shells filled with sea bass, and bay scallops in ricotta cheese sauce . . ."

"Yummy," Qing smacks her lips. "That's so incredible. I thought we would make some exotic Italian food today to amuse you. And now I am showing off in front of an Italian chef!" Qing laughs at herself. "But how did you transform yourself from a housekeeper into a scientist?"

"Oh, that's easy. Back in China, I was a professor of chemistry for ten years before going to New York. After I immigrated to Canada, I wanted to go back to my career and was lucky to find a laboratory job at the University of Toronto. Though it was a tedious and repetitive job that no one wanted, it offered me a stable income and that was what I needed to support my family. But you know, three years later came the budget cuts." She sighs.

"I love spaghetti, yummy, yummy," Alice says, running into the kitchen, "smells so good, Mum. I am very, very hungry." Suddenly Alice realizes it's not her mother standing by the stove. "Sorry, Rose, I thought you were my Mum."

"I wish," Rose remarks with a laugh, "but maybe I'm not a very good mother."

"Who says, your cooking smells delicious. Did your daughter call you Mum last night?" Alice asks abruptly.

Qing is surprised that her daughter still remembers the conversation they had on the sidewalk yesterday. She interrupts Alice softly: "We'll call you when dinner is ready."

With Alice gone, Qing takes the opportunity to ask Rose about her relationship with her daughter.

Rose left China to visit her uncle in New York in 1990. Her husband, Jin Wenbing, called her arrival in the Big Apple the first step in their family's strategic move, a step up, to the First World. He quoted an old Chinese saying, "What a drunk man wants is not always alcohol," indicating that visiting her uncle in New York was not the real purpose of Rose's trip, but an excuse to hide their family's real plan, to move to North America. When Rose was reluctant to leave their three-year-old daughter at home, Wenbing said to his wife seriously, "Listen to me, with every advancement comes a price tag, a sacrifice. But you see, what we need to pay for this huge step forward is actually very little. You just have to trust that I will take care of our daughter at home."

For the next three years Rose followed her husband's strategic plan step by step. As soon as she arrived in New York City, she took the second step—looking for work in the areas of labour shortage. She found out that many professional young families were looking for housekeepers. She called a few advertisers in a local newspaper and succeeded in landing a job for an Italian family in Manhattan. A year later she took the next important step—with her work experience as a housekeeper, she applied for immigration to Canada. It was another three years before she received her landing paper. She wasted no time in taking the final step of their plan—sponsoring her husband and daughter to come to Canada.

At the end of the fourth year, the ordeal of separation was over. She proudly told her friends who were still separated from their families in China, "You need a strategic planner like my husband." Rose stood at Pearson International Airport waiting for her husband and daughter to arrive, holding a bouquet of red roses, her favourite flower, after which she had chosen her English name when she landed in New York.

As the passengers pushed through the exit gate, Rose's eyes searched for her husband and daughter. Would her daughter still recognize her? Rose became anxious, but then she thought of their unbelievable achievement in only four years. Remembering the price her husband had given her earlier, and weighing it again in her mind at this moment, she was glad that the debt would be paid today. Rose smiled at the gate; finally, the moment she had been waiting for all these years! She raised the bouquet of red roses when Wenbing came out, pushing a loaded luggage cart and followed by a little girl. Rose rushed forward, bending down to her daughter. "Xiao Hong, my precious, let Mummy look at you, oh, you have grown up!" Rose opened her arms wide for her daughter to rush into her bosom. Tears rushed down her cheeks and she almost choked with excitement.

That is all she could ever remember of the episode. At that moment, something happened, or rather, nothing happened. Everything froze. The expected tearful hugging and kissing from her precious daughter never happened.

"I am your mother! Xiao Hong, take a look at me, this is Mummy!"

Rose stood there frozen in the same posture for a long time, her arms stretched, waiting to be recognized by her daughter. Other passengers walked by, embracing and kissing their relatives, but Xiao Hong turned her head away, refusing to look at her mother. The sweet baby voice that should have cried out "Mummy, Mummy" never came, as she tightly clenched her mouth. All Rose could hear was the humming of the florescent lights above her head. She finally gave up when her arms became stiff and numb.

"Xiao Hong must be shocked by the changes. She will be all right once we get home," Rose said to her husband, patting the girl's thin shoulders and wiping off her own tears quietly.

Rose started to read parenting books and magazines, seeking advice from other mothers. Following various suggestions, she bought Xiao Hong fashionable Canadian clothes, so the kids at school would accept her. In order to make the girl more popular, she even threw in a Chinese New Year's party for Xiao Hong's class. But no matter how hard she tried, she couldn't alter the stony coldness of her daughter towards her.

One day Xiao Hong said to Rose outside her school, "Please don't come to pick me up any more. I want my Ba Ba to pick me up."

"Why? Xiao Hong, why? I am your mother! I gave birth to you, you are the flesh that has dropped off my body!" She was nearly begging.

"You're a housekeeper!" Xiao Hong shouted at Rose, refusing to hold her hand. "My father is Party Secretary." The girl ran off, towards a traffic guard at the intersection, who held up a stop sign and escorted Xiao Hong across the street.

Rose, watching her daughter, broke down on the sidewalk. She had successfully carried out her husband's strategic landing plan to bring the family to North America, but she had forever lost her daughter in the process.

"Dinner is ready, Alice, can you set the table please?" Qing calls her daughter from the kitchen while Rose puts spaghetti in a big bowl and scoops out the thick sauce from the wok into another dish.

Qing became a single parent when Alice was only three years old. Back in China, where she had her divorce, for many years the law did not require the divorced man to pay child support if he didn't want future contact with his child. Alice's father chose to cut the relationship cold turkey and for good. Since then, Qing has been both mother and father to Alice.

"Table has been set, Mum," Alice reports to the kitchen. "Anything else I can do?"

"Bring the salad dressing, Italian vinaigrette."

"OK, Mum," replies Alice happily. Opening the refrigerator door, she picks up a bottle and checks the label. "Got it."

Rose stands there with the big serving dish in her hands. She watches the interaction between Alice and Qing with great pleasure. It reminds her of the two American boys in Manhattan where she was working as housekeeper. Like Alice, the boys always showed great interest in her cooking. The older boy, Michael, often came to the kitchen before dinner to help. During the summer season, Michael sometimes brought in one or two roses from the garden. "What colour do you like, Rose?"

"Every rose is beautiful, Michael sweetie, thank you." Rose gave

Michael a big hug, putting the cut roses in a vase on the windowsill. Sometimes she fantasized that Michael was related to her just like Xiao Hong, but only closer. A year later when Rose told the family she planned to move to Canada, Michael cried.

Now she lives with her own family, her husband and her own daughter. But she does not feel a member of her family. Her daughter looks down on her while her husband has little to do with her. They sleep in the same bed at different times of the day like two strangers working at the same job but on different shifts. Rose likes to go to bed around eleven at night and gets up around six-thirty in the morning. Wenbing, on the other hand, sits up all night to watch TV, sometimes until five o'clock in the morning. Many days they brush past each other, when one is going to bed and the other getting up, barely having anything to say.

Rose can't stop thinking about the two boys in New York, especially after her family reunion. She misses her intimate relationship with them and the days when she was their housekeeper.

At the dinner table, Alice tells her mother and Rose about events at school, anecdotes about her teachers and friends. Several times she switches the topic to comment on the food. "This is the best of the best spaghetti sauce I have ever had! My Mum always makes the best sauce, and today, Rose, you have made the best of the best. And I am going for the third serving."

Alice's words, like a summer breeze, blow away the clouds from Rose's s face. "I envy you, Qing, Alice is a nice kid."

"Yes, she is. You see, Rose, bringing up Alice by myself is not easy, but I believe that kids raised by single mothers sometimes can be emotionally healthier than those living with parents who are stuck in an unhappy marriage."

Rose stares at Qing, and then in a calm voice says, "Do you know why I walked out of my family last Saturday?"

Qing listens attentively.

"You know, there is only one washroom in our apartment, and it has been a problem ever since the family reunion. Every morning, Xiao Hong has to be the first one to use the washroom. Now that she is a teenager, she spends a lot more time in it than before. From showering to applying makeup, she sometimes occupies the washroom for an entire hour in the morning. Over the weekends, she usually gets up late, so last Saturday morning I went in the washroom first. But before I could finish my five-minute shower, she was kicking the door as if the house were on fire. 'Lao Ma Zi, get out of the washroom!' she shouted. I jumped out of the shower immediately and grabbed a towel to wrap around myself."

"Did she dare to call you *Lao Ma Zi*?" Qing asks in disbelief. She has heard the phrase before, but only in movies about the days before she was born. The phrase, meaning an old haggard woman, was used by the upper-class families for their female servants.

"Yes, she did. My own daughter called me *Lao Ma Zi*, can you believe it? And that was the last straw! I came out of the bathroom, quite shaken, and said to her, 'You ungrateful brat, listen to me. How dare you call your mother *Lao Ma Zi*! I am not ashamed to be a housekeeper. Why should you? Don't you forget this *Lao Ma Zi* sponsored you and your father to come to Canada! And this *Lao Ma Zi* is paying rent every month and buying food every day so that you can have this shelter.' I was very upset. I thought it was time to teach her a lesson about respect."

"Did she apologize?"

"No, she didn't. She didn't even say a word. She slammed the bathroom door in my face." Tears gushing from her eyes, Rose is shaking. "Qing, tell me what have I done wrong to deserve this emotional abuse from my own daughter?"

Qing passes a box of tissues to Rose. "What did your husband say about this?"

"He said if you plant a melon seed, you will harvest melons; but if you plant a thorn, you may have roses, or you may have only thorns."

"What did he mean by that?" Qing asks, puzzled.

"I don't know exactly. I suppose he meant fifty-fifty chance." Rose searches for words to paraphrase her husband's comments. "Some problems are inevitable in the process of immigration. I probably should have thought about it, knowing that we were to be separated for four years."

"And what kind of a role did your husband play, bringing up Xiao Hong to become such a monster child? Didn't he promise you he would look after the girl when you went to New York?"

"I asked him the same question. He said he did his duty. He did look after the girl, but somehow he has raised her to be a thorn without roses." Rose lets out a helpless sigh.

The two women fall silent. After a long pause, Rose concludes, "I didn't think I could take the abuse any more, so I left the house last Saturday afternoon."

"You did the right thing, Rose. Now, do you have any plans?"

"I am not going back to them unless they improve their behaviour. I mean unless they also want the family to exist as a family," says Rose seriously. Qing can see that her friend has weighed her decision many times and is aware of the price to be paid.

Rose has never gone back to live with her family. Not that she doesn't want to; she misses the home they had in China before she left for New York. But to Wenbing and Xiao Hong, Rose's absence from their present home on Huron Street feels more comfortable as they had become used to living without her prior to coming to Canada. That's why they have never asked Rose to move back. However, as the sponsor of the family, Rose continues to support her husband and daughter financially, paying their rent, leaving enough money for them to buy food, and sending gifts to Xiao Hong twice a year, on her birthday and at Christmas.

Later Rose rents a bachelor apartment for herself in the same residential area, hoping that she will run into her husband or daughter from time to time in the streets of this friendly neighbourhood.

In order to keep up with the expense of supporting two homes, Rose has been working at two jobs. She is a housekeeper during the day, and in the evenings she works as a telemarketer for a long-distance telephone company. Her life remains busy this way. One day she receives a brown envelope in the mail. A stack of postdated cheques she had signed for the house on Huron Street has been returned to her by the landlord. Only then does she realize that Wenbing and Xiao Hong have moved out from the rental house.

Holding the returned cheques in her hands, Rose shudders. Her blood turns cold. The image of herself at the airport with her arms stretched out long and wide, waiting to embrace her daughter, replays itself again and again in her mind. Rose forces herself to replace this tormenting image with another picture—eighteen years ago when Xiao Hong was still a toddler, Rose picked her up from kindergarten after work. Xiao Hong always greeted her mother at the door of the daycare with a sweet baby voice, "Mummy, Mummy," her small chubby hands clapping.

It has taken Rose half a year to find out what happened to her husband and daughter. Having received his Canadian citizenship and passport, Wenbing has gone to Hong Kong to make a living on his own. Xiao Hong, who finished her high school in just three and a half years, is at York University and living in residence.

Rose sits on the sofa with a cup of green tea. Sipping the tea slowly, she combs through her short hair with her fingers, letting out a series of deep sighs. Day after day, she sits there by herself sipping tea, sometimes for hours.

Then on New Year's eve, a simple truth dawns upon her. She realizes that she has accomplished her duty as a housekeeper to one more family, this time, her own family. The truth is that her own family is perhaps not much different from all the other families she has served.

"Rose, have you realized you are finally free?" She asks herself loudly.

"Yes, I am free! I am finally free! But free to do what?" She doesn't have answers to all her questions.

"Maybe, free to live my own life," she says hesitantly, and hears the answer in her head. Then she starts to repeat it loudly, and even more loudly, so that she can hear her own words echoing in the room.

The next time when Qing sees Rose again, it is probably three years later. It is an early summer afternoon, and Qing is shopping for vegetables in Chinatown. Suddenly, the sky darkens with black clouds; a gushing wind like a small twister picks up and blows Qing's hair all over her face. Pedestrians run towards the streetcar stop.

A formally dressed Chinese woman with a rouged face appears in front of Qing, smiling. "Qing, is that you?"

Qing focuses on the freshly blown hairdo tinted with red glow. "Hey, Rose! You look so pretty, so rosy, where are you heading to?"

"I've just come from my hairdresser's."

"Oh? You look like you are going to a party!"

"You have to wear a business suit when you go to a hairdresser. Otherwise they look down on you, thinking you are a housewife or a housekeeper, and they won't do your hair well." Rose talks with confidence.

"Oh, really? I thought it would be the opposite. One shouldn't wear good clothes to the hairdresser in case they get soiled, but anyway, I can't even remember the last time I visited a hairdresser!"

"Have to please myself sometimes," smiles Rose, her voice a musical tone. "Would you like to come for lunch tomorrow?"

Qing arrives at Rose's one-bedroom penthouse in a new condominium building near Scarborough Town Centre. When Rose opens the door, Qing thinks she is stepping into a different world—a garden of sunshine and tropical plants with large green leaves and strings of exotic orange flowers. Sitting on the glass tabletop is a transparent crystal bowl, in which some loose rose petals are floating on clear water. A rainbow of colours is reflected on the ceiling like magic.

In the bedroom, on top of a dresser, stands a large silver photo frame beside a vase of cut roses. The frame holds a small black-and-white picture. It was taken with an old Chinese camera some twenty years ago and shows a toddler stumbling along, her small chubby hands stretched out in front of her.

"One day, when Xiao Hong becomes a mother and has her own children, maybe she will come back to me," says Rose hopefully, standing beside Qing.

The two women step out to the rooftop garden. In the horizon, Lake Ontario is shimmering like a piece of silver silk. Down below them, street-lines cut the city into various shapes. Traffic moves quietly and slowly. There are trees and flowerbeds on the rooftop. In a couple of wooden planters, climbing roses stretch out their thorny stems, clinging onto the trellises against the exterior wall of the building, and arching out with clusters of flowers. Bees hover about the flowers.

African Lion Safari

KATHERINE WANG LEANS BACK comfortably against the backseat of the car. Her nine-year-old daughter, Lily, sits in the front passenger seat. Next to Katherine sits Susan Thomson, who knows both Katherine and John Lei, the driver. Early summer sunshine slants through the rear window, brightening the beige interior of the new Honda Accord.

"Beautiful day, isn't it?" Susan says. Soft music rises from the CD player on the dashboard.

"Indeed," John echoes from the driver's seat.

It is an hour's drive from Toronto to the African Lion Safari Park near Cambridge, west on Highway 401. Turning around under the seatbelt, Lily whispers to her mother over her small shoulders, "Mum, I like it."

"Shhhh," Katherine raises a finger, "like what?"

"This car," the girl whispers back.

"Uncle Lei might be able to take you out more often, right, John?" Susan says.

"Sure, Sue. Yes, Lily, maybe we can go to the Toronto Zoo next weekend." John tilts his head towards the girl.

Susan pulls Katherine's sleeve quietly. The two women exchange a look of mutual understanding. "Thank you, John, but I'm not sure about my schedule for next weekend." Katherine doesn't want to be obligated yet.

The car continues on the highway at a steady pace. Katherine scrutinizes the man sitting in front of her. John's bushy hair looks as if it was sprayed with pepper and salt, but more salt than pepper. Silver wire-framed sunglasses sit on his nose. For this first date arranged by Susan, John wears a beige sports jacket, which matches harmoniously with the interior of his car.

Suddenly a fresh smell of sprouting leaves and newly plowed soil floods into the car as Lily lowers her window an inch.

"Lily! Close the window please," Katherine sits up nervously in the backseat.

Lily reluctantly rolls up the window.

"It's OK," John smiles, "we're almost there."

The car slows down on the exit ramp. John's hands are firm on the wheel, and his back fits snugly into the seat. Katherine sits back, her arms crossing her chest.

Susan leans sideways to whisper in Katherine's ear, "Relax."

"Look, cars, so many cars!" Lily calls out cheerfully. There is a long queue of vehicles waiting at the gate of the Safari Park. John rolls down his window, his arm perches on the door. Lily immediately follows suit on her side. A warm breeze enters the car with the scent of wild animals and green vegetation, refreshing the passengers in the back seats.

Before this moment, Katherine has had no idea what "safari" actually means in Canada. Her first encounter with the word was when she was in university in China reading Earnest Hemingway's famous short story about an American couple shooting lions and buffalo in Africa. Since Susan told her about this trip, she has been wondering whether they will be chasing large animals on dusty roads.

"*Chang-jing-lu* ! *Chang-jing-lu* !" Lily shouts on top of her lungs.

"Look out! Lily!" John stretches out his arm to shield the girl from a young giraffe pushing its nose through the open window. The three adults scream with excitement while Lily puts her hands tenderly on the smooth skin of the long neck.

"Is *Chang-jing-lu* the Chinese name for giraffe?" Susan asks Katherine.

"You mean the long neck deer is called gee-rarf in English?" Katherine asks Susan at the same time.

"Hello, long neck deer! You are so beautiful!" The girl continues to talk to the giraffe in Chinese. The adults in the car also put their hands on the animal.

The car moves forward slowly. After this exciting moment with the giraffe at the gate, John asks Lily to roll up the window. They follow a long line of vehicles ahead. The two women in the backseat, still excited, now sit back to relax.

John is chatting with Lily about lions and tigers. Susan looks at Katherine, a faint smile on her lips, as if to say: You see, John would make a good father for Lily.

In the week following the safari, an unusual picturesque scene has preoccupied Katherine: a lion family resting on the slope under a big oak behind the wired fence. Katherine's mind focuses on the dreamy eyes of the lioness. She believes she communicated with the animal at the moment they made eye-to-eye contact. Relaxing beside the lioness is her male companion with his majestic pride and dignity as the king of the forest. Their two playful cubs are chasing each other around on the slope. In the calm contentedness of the lioness's eyes Katherine realizes a simple truth, which makes her jealous and has been bothering her since the trip.

Why can't she make herself as contented as the lioness, and her child a happier cub? Surely, she can. She is only forty-two years old, though not as young and pretty as she was at twenty-four when she first met Lily's father. She knows she is still capable of attracting men; occasionally some young men still wink at her boldly, but more often the middle-aged professional men throw her friendly smiles. Compliments from friends and strangers alike about her slender figure have given her enough confidence to believe that she should be able to find not only a handsome man, but also an established career man, one who has already made a success of his life.

"Mum, are we going out with Uncle John this weekend?" Lily interrupts Katherine's daydreaming. Maybe the girl is reading her mind, Katherine says to herself. "I want to go to the zoo. Uncle John has promised to take us to the zoo this Sunday."

Perhaps she should call Susan first, thinks Katherine. After all, Susan is their matchmaker.

"Hello, Sue?"

"Hey, Kathy, how's it going?" Susan asks cheerfully.

"Not much. I am just wondering about whether we should go out with John again this Sunday. You know, because of Lily, things get a bit complicated. The girl wants to go to the zoo with him, but I'm not so sure. I want to ask you for advice. How would you describe him in one sentence, Sue?"

"In one sentence, let me see, I would say John is a successful career man, and he looks like he could also be a devoted family man." Susan delivers her opinion cheerfully.

"Would you say you know him well, then? Do you think he is the right man for me?" Katherine shoots out her anxiety.

"Wow, what do you think I am? A fortune-teller?" Susan laughs. "I just thought you two are somewhat similar, one is a single mother, the other a single father, and each has a daughter. Plus you both are Chinese, maybe you want to meet. The rest is yours to explore and decide. I have nothing to do with it."

"I know, Sue." Katherine agrees. "By the way . . . there is a tradition back home in Shanghai, that if a matchmaker succeeds, she will receive ten pieces of pork hocks as a reward." Katherine can't help laughing at the idea of bringing ten pork hocks to Susan.

"What, what's that?"

"I'll bring you ten pork hocks if I end up with John," Katherine teases.

"That's a nice custom, but I am a vegetarian. Will you bring me ten veggie hocks made of tofu? Ha, ha, ha!"

"Sure! Ten veggie hocks," Katherine echoes. "A deal!"

"Good luck to you both!"

Katherine hasn't had a date since her divorce two years ago. Her ex-husband, Wu Gang, was a medical doctor in Shanghai. People in China respect medical professionals and sometimes call them soldiers-in-the-white-robe because of the battles they fight to save lives. Wu Gang cured Katherine of tuberculosis when she was twenty-three. In gratitude, the beautiful young patient developed love for the handsome doctor.

"You are my soldier-in-the-white-robe, my prince on the white horse!" she told him passionately. Soon after she was discharged from hospital, they walked hand-in-hand into cinemas and restaurants, each looking like a trophy for the other, a beautiful couple complementing each other and attracting admiration and gossip around them. Their romantic relationship quickly entered the next stage; one would think that an MD would know how to prevent an accident, but that was not the case. Katherine became pregnant shortly after she started dating her doctor.

"Don't worry. I'll fix it," Wu Gang said, patting her hand, when Katherine told him she had missed her last period. "Didn't I fix your TB?"

"Yes, you did. But this is different," Katherine said emotionally.

"It's quite common to have an abortion at this stage. It wouldn't even hurt you. I can do it for you myself if you prefer," he said in a consoling tone as if he were handing over a painkiller to one of his patients.

"No, definitely not!" Katherine's face was red and her voice hoarse from a sudden burst of anger. "This is my first pregnancy. I want to have this child."

Shouldn't he be happy that she was pregnant with his child? Didn't he love her dearly, as he had said? Katherine wanted to ask Wu Gang some questions, but she was afraid of bringing more stress to their tender relationship. Not wanting to face a sex scandal, which would tarnish the reputation of a medical doctor, they settled for a quick wedding.

Lily was born the next year. The young couple had been thrown into an exhausting parenthood for a few years before Katherine realized that something was wrong.

"How is the baby today?" Wu Gang asked her, as he did every evening when he returned home from work.

"Fine, she slept for two hours in the afternoon, drank 100 ml of milk, 100 ml orange juice, and 100 ml clear water, " Katherine reported to Wu Gang like a dietitian in a children's ward.

"Let me take your blood pressure." The doctor husband got the equipment out and stuck a stethoscope under the tightening wrap on Katherine's arm.

"Systolic 120, diastolic 80, pulse 75 per minute." He finished reading the mercury. "Any temperature? "

"No," Katherine answered, remembering the routine conversation she had had with Dr Wu when she was his patient.

"Good." After that Wu Gang would retire to the sofa in front of the TV until bed time.

"Where is the love in our relationship?" Katherine asked Wu Gang one day before he got up from his seat.

"Honestly, I don't know." His frankness shocked her.

In order to save their marriage, she raised the question of immigrating to Canada, where they could start all over again.

Two years later, their dream came true. In the early summer of 2000 they came to Toronto and rented a small two-bedroom apartment on the ground floor of a semidetached house among the working-class families in the city's east end.

The first six months in Canada went by like a long holiday. Then the leaves, once green, became colourful before falling on the sidewalks. Soon dry leaves gathered underneath the wheels and piled up in the gutters. One day, after returning from a job interview at a university laboratory, Wu Gang burst out at Katherine, "What made you believe that we could have a fresh start in Canada? "

Katherine was in the kitchen preparing dinner. She didn't respond, having known that the storm had to come one day.

"Without a doctor's licence, I am nobody. I'm not qualified to prac-tise medicine. But I can't even be a technician, not even an assistant technician. They said I am overqualified for the low-paying jobs."

Katherine didn't say a word as Wu Gang continued to pour out his disappointments. "In China, every year I was honoured as a model soldier-in-the-white-robe, but you thought that was propaganda. You thought Canada would offer us a better opportunity and a better life. To tell you the truth, right now I feel like a POW in this cold prison called Canada. Just take a look at me, after six months of job-hunting every day, I'm still unemployed. With both of us unemployed, how long do you think we can last financially?"

Outside the kitchen windows, the first winter snowstorm was sweeping across the streets with its mighty power. Katherine stood there wordlessly while water from the tap splashed on the vegetables in the sink. Pain was churning inside her stomach—her guilt at initi-ating their immigration to Canada. Maybe they should have stayed in China, separated or divorced by now; or maybe she should have taken the journey all by herself instead of sharing another major risk in life with Wu Gang. But six months in Canada was too soon for Katherine to make any decisions. She was not willing or ready to give up Wu Gang or Canada yet. She thought she would persuade her husband to try a bit harder and for a little longer, maybe even to consider a trade.

Standing there at the kitchen sink, Katherine made an offer to Wu Gang. "Listen, I have an opportunity for you. I will find a job, maybe two part-time jobs, to support you and Lily if you want to go back to school."

Wu Gang looked at Katherine with disbelief; this small woman, once his patient, who later became his wife, had just said something incredibly brave, as if she were facing another life-threatening battle.

"In that case," he said hesitantly, "I will let you convince me one more time that I will be able to start a new career all over again." After pausing for some time, he murmured to himself as if to cover up his embarrassment, "After all, new immigrants have to adjust to the Canadian job market."

Wu Gang registered at George Brown College for a two-year program to become a certified chef while Katherine started working at three part-time jobs. Her daytime job was as a mover at the Canadian National Exhibition, her task to set up or take down trade shows. At night, she became a sewing-machine operator working on button-holes in a garment factory near Chinatown, on Spadina and Queen Street West. Over the weekends, she put on a tall white paper hat to work at a bakery in Little Italy on College Street, making twisted French baguette, hard-crusted Italian bread, and various sweet muffins that she had never heard of before coming to Canada. Suddenly, their family life changed dramatically. For better or for worse, there seemed to be a purpose in everything.

One late afternoon, Katherine was making fried rice in the kitchen before rushing to her evening job. Wu Gang came in. "I think we should follow the official Canadian food chart."

"What?" Pouring oil into the smoky wok, Katherine had no clue what her husband was talking about.

"I say, we should eat a healthier diet by following the official Canadian food chart." Wu Gang repeated.

Katherine looked at her husband, who was holding up a colour chart that showed a diagram in the shape of a pyramid. Wu Gang continued, "For every daily intake of food, there should be some dairy products, such as cheese . . ."

"Is this a law?" Katherine interrupted. She thought she had heard the word "official."

"Not a law, but it's recommended to Canadians for maintaining good health," Wu Gang explained.

The stove was on high heat. Katherine's hand was hanging in the air holding a metal stirrer. She smelt burnt rice.

"Bullshit!" Katherine couldn't believe she had just uttered a word she had overheard from fellow movers.

"What? Did you just swear at me? When did you learn to swear?" Wu Gang said, startled.

"I said bullshit. If there is such a great official health food chart, why do we see so many fat Canadians? As for our family, if following the official food chart is so important to you, and since you are studying to become a licenced chef, why don't you fix a healthy dinner for us sometime?"

She had snapped back at him for the first time in their marriage.

What did he think she had been eating in between her jobs? Following some kind of official food chart? She wanted to laugh at Wu Gang's naive bookworm theory. Moving furniture all day long, her body needed a lot of calories for energy. She had fed her hunger with hotdogs, french fries, sweet danishes, muffins, and the $2.99 Chinese combo in the basement of a Chinatown food court. Did Wu Gang really care about her diet or her health?

After her outburst, Wu Gang ceased talking to his wife about food. In fact he seldom ate dinner at home with Katherine and Lily. They didn't see each other much throughout the day. At night, they slept next to each other like two strangers sharing a subway bench.

Two years later, Wu Gang graduated as an award-winning chef. A week after his graduation, he informed Katherine that he had decided to move to Vancouver where he would make a fresh start. From this point on, he would seek an official separation from her.

"You scoundrel!" Katherine didn't know how to express her anger. She blamed herself for putting on weight and for becoming less interesting to him, especially after she quit her evening ESL class in order to work at the garment factory. For two years, she had been completely preoccupied by her daily routine as the sole breadwinner of their family. She liked the word, breadwinner, which she had learned at the bakery. Had she ignored the changes in her relationship with her husband? Of course she had. She had stopped using the cliché, soldier-in-the-white-robe, and he had not checked her blood pressure ever since he started his training to become a chef.

The day Wu Gang walked out on Katherine, she passed out inside the elevator while moving a stack of chairs on a dolly. When the elevator door closed, she felt the whole world caving in on her. She wanted to call for help, but no sound came. Then her knees went soft. She leaned on the wall of the elevator like some old rags on a stick, a scarecrow. While the metal cage was descending faster and faster, she collapsed into a bottomless abyss of darkness as if being sucked into a black hole.

Katherine lets out a deep sigh as she looks out of the kitchen window. The branches of an old crabapple tree leaning over the walls of the neighbour's backyard have suddenly become covered with pink blossoms. What a lustrous sight! But how strange, she didn't even know it was a flower tree until this spring. She has also just realized that grass suddenly turns green overnight after a spring shower. Under the branches of the blooming crabapple, Katherine thinks she sees the lioness again, sitting on the grass leaning against the lion king. She exchanges a look with the female creature whose eyes gleam back at her ever so meaningfully.

Sunday morning, John stops his car in front of the semidetached small house where Katherine and Lily live. After double-checking the street number, he gently presses the doorbell. Katherine is standing behind the counter, wrapping up the last sandwiches. She wears an apron over a summer dress; her long hair is rolled up and pinned onto the back of her head, revealing her slender neck. A plastic cooler sits on top of the counter.

"Mom, Uncle John is here!" Lily cries happily and rushes to the door.

"Hi, Lily! Hi Kathy." John greets the mother and daughter cheerfully.

"I'm ready to go to the zoo!" Lily is holding John's hand.

Katherine smiles, washes her hands under the tap. "I've made some tuna sandwiches for lunch." She looks at John, placing three apples, three small yogurt containers, and a two-litre bottle of soft drink into the cooler. "All set to go!"

Watching John as he puts the cooler inside the trunk of the car, and as Lily gets into the front passenger seat, Katherine feels a surge of warmth spreading through her body. She quickly dismisses the feeling, and laughs at herself quietly for being emotionally needy.

Katherine sits in the back seat where she sat last Sunday. She seems to feel more comfortable now in John's car. She notes that he is wearing light beige again, a short-sleeve sports shirt, and khaki pants with a Gap label on the pocket. This perfect colour coordination, light beige being a soft neutral colour that accommodates other colours, must mean that John is a man of discipline.

"I like the colour of your car," Katherine comments, hoping to start a conversation. Lily's pink dress and her own floral summer dress brighten the mood in the soft interior of the vehicle.

"I am glad to hear that," says John, tilting his head. "Do you like it too, Lily?"

"Of course, I said it last time," Lily answers firmly.

"When did you buy this car?" Cautiously, Katherine asks a money-related question. She has heard that asking money questions is like stepping into a minefield when dating. However, since she wants to know him, she has to take the risk.

"Oh, it's not mine. This is a company car. My boss lets me drive it. Isn't that nice?"

"Oh . . . a company car, and a brand new one. Your boss must be very fond of you." Not all employees get to drive a company car, she thinks. John must be well established at work.

"I hope so," says John with a smile as neutral as the beige colour of the company car.

Katherine leans back against the soft fabric, closing her eyes for a minute, imagining the lioness leaning against the lion king. Though it is only her second time meeting him, she feels somewhat relaxed.

The car stops at the parking lot of the Toronto Zoo.

Once inside, the two adults follow Lily, who is running ahead of them like a tourist guide. "Monkeys! Uncle John, come here! Mum, this way!" Lily pushes through the crowd to the front.

"Take it easy, Lily," Katherine shouts at the girl. When she walks side by side with John away from the crowd, she lets out one of her many questions in a soft whisper, "John, what happened to your previous marriage?" She regrets it immediately, remembering that Susan has told her John's wife died.

"Oh . . ." John looks a little alarmed, but quickly gives Katherine a factual statement, "My wife died during an asthma attack two years ago. Now I live with my twenty-year-old daughter, who is attending York University."

John's wife died the same year that Katherine's husband walked out on her, she reflects. So they both had bad luck that year. "Why didn't you bring your daughter today?" she asks gently and chidingly.

"Reindeer! Mum, hurry up!" Lily stands at the low fence over a green pasture, patting a reindeer with one hand while waving with the other. Any passerby would think they are a family. Katherine smiles at John as they both run down the slope to join Lily.

"I did ask her this morning, but she said she was too busy, maybe next time." John didn't forget Katherine's question.

"I heard tuition is going up in September." Katherine thinks now she has more to consider if she is going to develop a relationship with John. Together they will be a family of four, with two daughters.

"I-N-G Direct Lion Exhibit," Lily reads slowly from a plaque by the side of the road. "What does that mean?"

John walks over. "I see, ING Direct probably has adopted the lions."

"What is ING Direct?" Katherine and Lily question simultaneously.

"Oh, it's a Dutch bank doing business in Canada. The bank's logo has a lion," answers John.

"Why didn't the bank adopt a reindeer for a pet?" Lily comments curiously.

Further down the road, they see another sign, "Imperial Oil Siberian Tiger Exhibit." Katherine feels somewhat sad that large fierce zoo animals are sponsored by powerful corporations. She dislikes the

ING Direct lions. These lions don't look the same as her lioness, the lion king, and their happy cubs at the African Lion Safari Park.

At the end of the day, John says he and his daughter would like to invite Katherine and Lily to brunch next Sunday.

Around noon on Sunday, Katherine and Lily arrive at the second floor of Bright Pearl Restaurant in Chinatown for brunch. Katherine likes the restaurant, and she is delighted that John has chosen Bright Pearl out of the dozens of other Chinese restaurants along Spadina Avenue. She feels more elevated when she sees the two stone lions sitting majestically in front of the restaurant's side door, as if welcoming her. Both she and Lily have looked forward to today's dim sum brunch because they will meet John's daughter, Yuanyuan, for the first time. As they step into the dining room, they see a girl stand up as soon as John rises to greet them. The young woman is taller than Katherine, wearing a tight T-shirt and hip jeans showing her navel.

"Aunty. Little Sister," Yuanyuan says, following the Chinese tradition.

At the table, Lily sits beside Yuanyuan, and Katherine next to John. When the waiters and waitresses push the wheeled carts along, Yuanyuan immediately gets up to order dim sum items from the hot steamers for everyone. John pours out light green tea from a white porcelain teapot into four small, white teacups. Katherine watches Yuanyuan and John perform in perfect ritual harmony as if they have done this many times. When John places a cup of tea in front of his daughter, Yuanyuan uses her index finger to drum on the table a few times. Lily follows Yuanyuan, making finger-drumming noise on the table as well. Katherine senses this must be a local or southern Chinese custom to show appreciation, so she does the same.

"You are all welcome," smiles John.

"Do you like school?" Lily asks Yuanyuan.

"Of course," Yuanyuan answers without hesitation, as if to say what a strange question. "Do you?" she throws the question back at Lily.

With a mischievous smile, Lily answers in English, "Horses and tigers."

"What?" Yuanyuan gazes at Lily, and then bursts out laughing, "Oh, I got it. You mean *ma-ma-hu-hu*, so so."

Katherine can't believe that Lily would give such a playful but misleading answer, but she doesn't think Yuanyuan is really amused. She watches the young woman's perfectly shaped eyebrows twitch up and down as if to say to Lily, You probably aren't a very good student.

Yuanyuan puts vinegar in her plate, and then dips dim sum in it; she dips almost everything, from steamed shrimp dumpling, ribs, squid, to phoenix's feet and even stir-fried noodles. John says he likes traditional Cantonese taste, with fresh vegetables and seafood in their original flavour. He doesn't even need dressing for his salad. Katherine and Lily, on the other hand, prefer soy sauce and hot chili pepper—Sichuan-style spicy.

How are we ever going to juggle all these different tastes in a single wok? Katherine wonders. At the end of the brunch, she has invited John and Yuanyuan to her home for dinner the following Sunday.

The week goes by fast. It's Sunday afternoon again, and Katherine is setting the table for four, when she feels a need to talk to Susan.

"Hello, Sue."

"Hey, Kathy, how's it going?" Susan always sounds cheerful and encouraging.

"Pretty good, I mean, it's going well." Katherine smiles at the receiver, putting down napkins and chopsticks beside each plate. "I'm having them over for dinner tonight. John and his daughter Yuanyuan."

"I'm pleased to hear that. So should I be expecting my veggie hocks soon?" She laughs.

"I hope so, Sue. Do you think I can ask John about his plans for the future?" Katherine has been preoccupied with some urgent questions since last Sunday's brunch.

"I don't know, it all depends on how comfortable you are with each other. How long has it been since the trip to the African Safari?"

asks Susan.

"It's been two months and one week, sixty-eight days altogether," Katherine answers without a second thought.

"My goodness, has it been that long? You certainly have the right to ask personal questions," agrees Susan.

"You see, we are middle-aged adults seeking partners. I don't think we should waste more time and money going to more parks and restaurants. I feel we need to talk seriously about family and other matters, what do you think?"

"That'd be nice, and it's certainly the next stage."

"Sue, do you know, by any chance, how much John makes from work?" Katherine bursts out with one of her burning questions.

"Oh, that, I don't know. I guess around 70k annually as an IT manager," Susan says, hesitating. "You should really ask him yourself. Anyway, I wish you good luck. And have a great dinner tonight."

Katherine realizes that every time she tries to get some specific information about John from Susan, her friend instantly shortens their conversation. John hasn't offered any details about how he makes a living, neither has he asked Katherine about her financial situation. She doesn't understand why asking a financial question is such a taboo in the West. Don't people want to know what they are getting into before they become serious about each other? How can anyone separate finance from romance?

Katherine thinks the coming dinner may well be another landmark test for their relationship. She wishes she had learned a few fancy dishes from her ex-husband, the award-winning chef. After her divorce from Wu Gang, she and Lily have been living on simple meals. They love spaghetti, chow mein mixed with vegetables and slices of barbecue pork or tender chicken breast, and their favourite fried rice would have bits of barbecue pork, scrambled eggs, and green onions flavoured with light soy sauce and hot chili powder. Sometimes Katherine throws in frozen peas and corn to enrich the taste and enhance the colour. Chinese cuisine requires colour, smell, and taste be simultaneously present to attract the eater. She thinks her best fried rice has certainly achieved all three qualities. But she can't serve fried rice to their special guests because it is considered a casual dish. She would become a laughing stock for John and Yuanyuan to make fun of afterwards. In the end, she decides to try a northern menu, different from Cantonese cuisine, although she hasn't made these dishes for a long time.

Sunday evening when the guests are at the door, the kitchen is full of hot steam. The damp foggy atmosphere seems to conceal a big secret to the visitors.

"Smells good," John says encouragingly, laying down a bottle of red wine on the counter. Yuanyuan sniffs around, trying to figure out what this aunty has been cooking.

Around eight o'clock, Katherine is ready to serve. First, she puts down four cold dishes: cold cucumber, cold bean sprouts, fried peanuts, and thin slices of pork ears. Then she brings out two plates of hot steamed buns.

"I love steamed buns," Lily announces as she sits down at the table.

"So do I," Yuanyuan echoes.

John pours out two glasses of red wine for the adults.

The two girls try to pick up fried peanuts with their chopsticks and put them inside their mouths. They giggle loudly when the peanuts fall off.

Katherine is relieved. Her northern menu, after all, offers a lot of fun.

During the course of the dinner, she observes John and Yuanyuan closely. Their chopsticks have visited the bean spouts only once—"too garlicky for me," Yuanyuan comments. For some reason, the young guest hasn't touched the glass of chilled Coke that Lily has poured out for her. Instead, she asks Lily for cold water. After she has tasted every dish once, Yuanyuan picks up a steamed bun. But as soon as she bites into it, her facial muscles stop moving as though she has just lost a tooth. She then closes her mouth tightly while examining the filling in the bun before putting it down on her plate.

"What's wrong, Yuanyuan?" Katherine asks the girl, hoping she doesn't sound reproachful.

"I'm not sure I like the filling," answers Yuanyuan with a grin. "It's bitter."

"Nonsense, Yuanyuan," John scolds the girl with a harsh tone Katherine hasn't heard before.

"Mum, it *is* bitter!" Lily spits out what's inside her month onto the plate, putting down her bun as well. "What's in the filling?" Lily asks loudly.

"It's bitter melon with minced pork, a recipe from northern China," Katherine explains, "but I have boiled the bitter melon first to get rid of the bitterness."

"Oh, . . ." John looks at Katherine wordlessly. Disappointment appears on his face as if to say you should have known better. "Next time, just use minced pork with green onion and ginger, flavoured with salt, pepper and a pinch of sugar, it would be a lot easier to make and guaranteed to taste great."

Katherine can't believe this! Without hesitation, this man has just pulled out a recipe from his sleeve as if he were an award-winning chef.

Suddenly Katherine also realizes that she has been humiliated by her guests. She needs to defend her recipe because it belongs to a different tradition. "Bitter melon is really good for your health especially in the summer," she argues. "The first bite might taste a bit bitter, but after several bites you won't mind it at all. Actually, you might even like the taste."

"Ugh ugh, "the girls shake their heads. They ask to be excused, leaving on their plates two crescent-shaped buns each with a single bite.

John raises his wine glass at Katherine. "Don't worry, I don't mind the taste. Cheers."

Katherine begins to think that forming a family with this man and his daughter is going to be a real challenge. Not only would the two girls gang up on her, as young women usually do when they share space with an older woman, but also John and Yuanyuan, as an old alliance, could make her life miserable.

"Would you like to come to my house for dinner next Sunday?" John issues an invitation at the end of the dinner. "Let Yuanyuan make some southern dishes for you and Lily."

Before saying good night at the door, John picks up Katherine's right hand for the first time and puts a light kiss on the back.

The following week, after coming back from work, Katherine finds herself sitting in the kitchen a lot. Outside the window, the neighbour's crabapple tree has stretched its branches against the blue sky. The pink blossoms are all gone; now the tree is covered with green foliage and small fruits. Her mouth feels as if she has bitten into a sour crabapple.

Below the branches, Katherine searches for her elusive lioness. But the creature is no longer there, nor are the lion king and their two cubs. Katherine wonders if perhaps starting a new family at this age is only a dream, just as it is for Francis Macomber in Hemingway's short story, in which the doomed man hopes to reestablish his relationship with his wife through a safari trip.

"Do you know a new Batman movie, Lily?" Katherine asks her daughter Sunday morning.

"You mean *Batman Begins*?" Lily is surprised that her mother is interested in an action movie.

"Yes, that's it. Do you want to see it?"

"Sure," Lily answers happily.

At four o'clock in the afternoon, instead of getting ready to go to John's house for dinner, Katherine and Lily set off for the cinema at Yonge and Dundas. Before locking up the door, Katherine throws a quick glance at the answering machine on the kitchen counter. The little red light is not on.

At 5:30, the mother and daughter are sitting down comfortably in the movie theatre, having a large bag of buttered popcorn, waiting for the movie to start. Katherine is not totally at ease with her decision.

She knows she still has time to make a phone call to prevent the unnecessary frustration for the other household. But she can't think of a reasonable excuse to step out of the cinema right now as the movie has already started. With a sigh, she sits back and decides to let their no-show do the killing. There is no point in prolonging a hopeless relationship, is there? It's better to end it sooner than later.

By the time the movie is over, it is around 8 P.M. Katherine and Lily, holding hands, stroll down Yonge Street aimlessly, passing street vendors selling flags and hotdogs, and a dozen street artists, who ask them to sit down for a charcoal sketch. The mother and daughter walk away from the busy intersection and enter MacDonald's for dinner as they usually do on occasions like this.

At about 10:30 P.M., Katherine and Lily finally arrive home. They haven't heard the telephone. There is no message for Katherine to check either. At the other place, for three hours, John and Yuanyuan have waited anxiously for their guests to arrive, so that they can cook their delicate southern cuisine. The fresh seafood and vegetables sitting on the countertop to be cooked upon the guests' arrival have changed colour a long time ago.

After the "wicked weekend," Katherine feels a little nervous on Monday and Tuesday. By Wednesday evening when their phone hasn't rung even once, she feels somewhat relieved and then annoyed. Her life has returned to what it was like before their trip to the African Safari two and a half months ago.

Katherine and Lily have gone back to having their favourite fried rice for dinner, even on the weekends. In the evening, sitting down in the kitchen by herself and pondering over the recent events, she feels at times regretful for what she has done to John and Yuanyuan, but at other times she feels angry with John. The man certainly has too much pride, as most men do. Why can't he simply pick up the phone and give her one more call? Doesn't he want to make sure that she and Lily were safe that night? Maybe he doesn't really care about them. Then why should she care about him? If they had developed a relationship,

John could have turned out to be Wu Gang Number Two. She concludes she has made the right decision at the right time. Katherine feels her anxiety lift at the thought that she has just avoided another major disaster in her life.

There will be no more dates for the coming Sundays. Katherine feels a tremendous relief. She needs to give Susan a call about the ending of her romance. Unlike Mrs Macomber, Katherine is not afraid to admit that she has killed the possibility of having John as her husband.

"Sue, I killed it."

"What? . . . Oh you did? I thought . . . ," her friend stammers.

"I know," Katherine says after a pause. "And I'm sorry . . . you were very close to getting the veggie hocks."

At that, Susan bursts out laughing. "I don't think so, not after you told me he hasn't opened up to you at all. It's a pity really, because he could make a good father for Lily, but he had to be a good lover for you first."

Katherine sits by herself in the same position in the kitchen, facing the windows and pondering over her life. She thinks John could well be a traditional family man, whose sole interest in life is to make regular mortgage payments, pay his daughter's tuition, and wait to receive his company benefits and Canada pension. There is nothing wrong with having a nice man like John as a husband, but Katherine just knows she wouldn't be totally happy with him. She longs to meet someone who is a little more adventurous, someone who doesn't always wear the boring beige colour.

Looking around her and thinking about her own life, Katherine smiles. Her index finger drums on the tabletop, and she feels thankful. After all, she has created a good life for herself and Lily. She is proud that she has worked hard to support her family ever since she landed in Canada. Although she doesn't own a house or a car yet, financially she is debt-free. She has also gone back to the ESL classes on Saturdays. And now her English has progressed to the intermediate level. Since their divorce, Wu Gang has been sending her $500 every month for child support, which pays more than half the rent. Katherine makes $1200 monthly at the National Exhibition. Maybe it isn't much compared to what people make in the IT industry, but because of her diligent housekeeping, she manages to put away some savings into her bank account, including a small RRSP investment. Every other week, she and Lily go out for a movie or an outing using public transportation to get around. Comparing her worry-free life with those of many single mothers in the city who live on welfare or who can't make both ends meet, Katherine is proud of her financial independence. She really has nothing to complain about other than occasionally feeling lonely. But loneliness is a common experience in a big city like Toronto. It is certainly less of a problem than having to live with an abusive or an indifferent spouse.

Katherine gets up to open the window. The setting sun has painted the horizon in bright yellow, orange, scarlet, and purple colours. Across the sky, crimson clouds are moving with the wind. At the far edge of the earth, she suddenly sees her lioness standing magnificently above the clouds all by herself; the creature's bright eyes are shining like rubies. Suddenly, her lioness starts to chase the high wind and the setting sun.

"A beautiful sunset forecasts a thousand-mile journey," Katherine utters an old Chinese saying. She unlocks the deadbolt lock and swings the front door wide open. For the first time in her life, she is confident that she can travel the thousand-mile journey by herself.

A Wanton Woman

YI MEI HASN'T TALKED to Ai Hua for three years, not since her last visit to China in the summer of 2001. Tonight, sitting in her apartment in the west end of Toronto, and listening to an early December snow landing quietly on the street, she suddenly feels compelled to talk to her friend.

They were bosom friends twenty years ago, living in the same neighbourhood by the side of the Yangtze River. At that time, both were in their early thirties and divorced with a child each. Yi Mei was pale and thin, and Ai Hua dark and stout. Yi Mei was a high school teacher; Ai Hua worked as a drafting assistant at an architectural firm. Many hot summer nights they sat by the river, cracking roasted sunflower seeds and fantasizing about romantic men while their kids played on the beach.

Yi Mei still likes cracking roasted sunflower seeds. Except that now she does it all alone in her rental apartment. She doesn't spit out the shells directly from her mouth any more, afraid of making a mess on the carpet. Instead she holds a seed with her left thumb and index finger, and places it between her front teeth; after the teeth and tongue have worked the kernel out, she puts the broken shells into the waste-basket at her feet.

Pulling the desk drawer open, Yi Mei takes out a long-distance phone card. She dials the automatic operator. After a prompt, she enters the pin number, a set of ten digits. "You have five dollars," the automatic operator announces. She enters a long string of fifteen numbers. "You can talk for 3 hours and 20 minutes," the operator continues in a flat voice. What an invention! Yi Mei is grateful every time she uses a long-distance phone card. She remembers that when she first came to Canada some ten years ago, calling China was a luxury. Now she can afford to call China almost any time. Waiting for her friend's phone to ring on the other side of the earth, she teases herself, "It would be a miracle to actually talk to her."

Yi Mei has tried calling Ai Hua from time to time over the past three years. Each time she has called, Ai Hua's phone rings, but she is never home. Like most people in China, she doesn't have an answering machine or voice mail, so Yi Mei can't leave a message. This time, when the phone rings. Yi Mei places the receiver close to her left ear, holding her breath while counting the rings. Once, twice, three times, four, five . . . suddenly, a voice, loud and puffing, hits her eardrum with an incredible volume, "Who is this?"

Yi Mei is too excited to identify the voice immediately. Isn't it a custom in China to say "*Wei*" when one picks up the phone? But she will just pretend it is Ai Hua. So she answers, "It's me, Hua, recognize my voice?" She speaks slowly, giving the other side time to respond.

"Who? Who's this?" The voice hesitates, less irritated than before; suddenly, it bursts out from the receiver. "Is that you, Mei? Is that actually *you*, Mei?"

"It's me, Hua! It is Mei!" Yi Mei's voice quivers. Only family members and close friends in China call her by her first name. Her anxiety comes down. Ai Hua speaks with a northern accent, rapid and smooth, like a clear brook gushing out from behind a rock in the forest.

"How I miss you, Mei! It's been three years and we haven't talked." Ai Hua breaks down. Yi Mei holds the receiver away from her left ear, while dabbing a Kleenex at her own eyes. Ai Hua's voice continues to flow out from the telephone, "I dream of you, I wake up crying to myself, Mei, you don't miss me this much."

Yi Mei waits for Ai Hua to finish with her complaints. She doesn't tell Ai Hua how many times she has tried to reach her.

"Mei, there is something I've wanted to tell you since your last visit." Ai Hua suddenly sounds quite businesslike.

"What's that?" Yi Mei is alert. Her mind quickly searches for possible topics. She hopes her friend is not going to tell her that she plans to re-marry her ex-husband.

"I want to ask you," Ai Hua speaks earnestly, "would you please delete the image you have about me from your head? I am *not* a wanton woman."

"What, Hua, what . . . are you talking about? What do you want me to do?"

"Mei, I am not a wanton woman! So please delete the image you have about me from your head." Ai Hua repeats firmly and emotionally.

"Hua, please, . . . I didn't say you were, did I?"

"But in the short story you've drafted about the three divorced women, you believe I am a loose woman. I am sorry, I don't like that image." Anxiously, Ai Hua continues, "Has the story been published?"

"That one, yes, it has. Three years ago." Yi Mei slows down apologetically. "Hua, listen to me, it's only a story, you know, the characters are fictional, nothing personal."

Yi Mei recalls an evening of her last visit. They were sitting on the old sofa in her parents' apartment, cracking roasted sunflower seeds. Ai Hua wanted to know what Yi Mei had written in her forthcoming book. Yi Mei said she could translate a short story she was working on for her friend. So Ai Hua sat back, listened attentively, gradually forgetting the sunflower seeds in her hand, while Yi Mei translated the short story from English to Chinese. After Yi Mei finished reading the story, Ai Hua asked, "Is the story about me?"

"All I can say is that you are a prototype only, " answered Yi Mei.

"I see. But still, it's about me. You are recreating me," Ai Hua remarked. "But you have picked only a few episodes from my life, and that's not fair. If you want to write about me, you should write a complete story about my life."

"I wish, I wish one day I could do that," answered Yi Mei, laughing at her friend's demand.

That was three years ago, so why is Ai Hua preoccupied with the character of that old story? Yi Mei has no idea. Her friend certainly has an incredible memory.

"But if this is all you can do about my image, it makes me sad whenever I think about it," Ai Hua says emotionally on the other end of the telephone line. "How can you hold such a deprecating opinion about me? I always think about you as a sister, but you have described me as sexy, adventurous, and tomboyish, I really don't like it."

Yi Mei's earlier excitement has been replaced by defensiveness. Holding the receiver tightly, she hears herself speaking seriously like a literary critic or a university professor. "Hua, please let me explain the meaning of these words to you. First, 'sexy' is a compliment and refers to the femininity of the character. She enjoys being a woman and makes it clear to others. Second, 'adventurous' is not a bad word either. It means she is brave, decisive, and willing to take risks, perhaps somewhat nontraditional for her gender. And thirdly, being tomboyish suggests that she is both feminine and masculine, you know, and modelled after you, the character is almost perfect."

"Perfect for who?" Ai Hua argues.

Yi Mei is silent. After a long pause, she says, "Perfect for Western readers, I suppose." She admits the readership she has in mind. "Maybe for the younger generation of Chinese readers as well. Since China is undergoing dramatic changes."

This time, Ai Hua becomes wordless. She tries to follow Yi Mei's description of the character. Perhaps she should accept such a contemporary woman as her model. She holds the image in her head for a few minutes, but it starts to blur. Ai Hua says, "In traditional Chinese culture, you don't call a woman sexy unless you mean wanton, lustful, lecherous, lascivious, you know what I mean. And what you're really implying is that she is loose, like a whore . . . "

"Oh, no, no, hold on, Hua," Yi Mei interrupts, "I only said sexy."

"But what the word implies is what the reader gets. And the word 'adventurous,'" Ai Hua says sadly, "for a divorced woman, unfortunately, can only mean risky and dangerous." She knows the prejudices only too well, having been a divorced woman most of her adult life. "Mei," Ai Hua's voice drops low, "I forgot, you have already become westernized."

"I'm sorry, Hua."

They hang up.

Yi Mei doesn't know why she has to apologize. It is certainly a Western custom.

With a bitter taste in her mouth, Yi Mei grabs a handful of sunflower seeds from the package on the small coffee table. One after another, she cracks the seeds like mad and spits out broken shells from her mouth, forgetting her carpet, as if she were sitting by the Yangtze River. Bits and pieces of broken shells fall down on the carpet around her feet. Yi Mei looks at the floor; she simply cannot stop thinking about Ai Hua.

Ai Hua has married and divorced the same man twice, the father of her son. "How could you remarry the same man you divorced?" Yi Mei asked her friend three years ago.

"For love, I thought I could still love him," Ai Hua answered. "I wanted to give him a second chance, because he said the young woman at work had seduced him."

"Then, what made you divorce him for the second time?" Yi Mei continued.

"Two years after our remarriage, he told me another young woman had seduced him," Ai Hua's voice was loaded with pain.

"Why didn't you believe him this time?" Yi Mei really wanted to know why forgiveness didn't save Ai Hua's marriage.

"Because the woman committed suicide," Ai Hua sounded sad and tired as if she were carrying a weight. "I decided to divorce him that same day."

After Ai Hua's second divorce, she met an engineer, a married man with a wife and child. This time, she became an unpopular, third party in another couple's marriage. They kept a secret relationship going for three years.

"Why did you break up with the engineer?" Yi Mei asked Ai Hua during her last visit.

"I was pregnant with his child," she answered without hesitation. "I had to make a decision. So one day, I decided to talk to his wife."

"Oh, no, you didn't? Why did you want to get his wife involved in this mess? Don't you think that was a bit too much?" Yi Mei felt compelled to find out her friend's motivation, so she continued, "What did you say to her?"

"I said she had the right to throw me out or to take me to the police," Ai Hua paused to catch her breath, "but if not, I wanted to know what she was going to do about the situation. She asked me what situation. I pointed at my belly and told her, 'I'm seven weeks pregnant with your husband's child. And I have a decision to make. If you still love your husband, you should get him back to the family. But if not, I am here to ask you to set him free.'"

"What did she say?"

"She didn't say a word. Like him, she's also a coward." After Ai Hua's unexpected visit, the engineer was suddenly transferred to another company. And she was left alone to lick her wounds and bear her shame. "I had no choice but to abort the fetus." Ai Hua's voice was so low that Yi Mei could hardly hear it.

A year after the engineer left Ai Hua, she met a young musician in the city's First Jazz Bar. Though ten years her junior, the young man fell madly in love with her and swore he would marry no one but Ai Hua. For some time, Ai Hua refused to believe this puppy love would last. However, after two years she gave in to his pursuit. She resigned from her job and together they opened their own Yangtze Jazz Bar. On the grand opening night, his band played for their wedding. A year later, Ai Hua gave birth to a baby boy, her second son. Her personal life again became a hot topic in the neighbourhood, except that this time it was a fairy tale.

After two years of a happily married life, Ai Hua's young husband was diagnosed with acute leukemia. Yi Mei remembers going to the hospital with Ai Hua to visit her sick man during her trip three years ago. Wrapped up in hospital garments, the young musician was pale like paper and too weak to talk. Yi Mei couldn't imagine him as the hot-blooded guitarist whose passionate love and music had melted Ai Hua's cool rational analysis.

But this was three years ago. Is Ai Hua's husband still alive? Yi Mei wonders.

Yi Mei's hand has been going in and out of the bag of roasted sunflower seeds on the coffee table for almost an hour. The broken shells on the carpet have gradually piled up underneath her feet like loose sand on the beach. Like a robot, Yi Mei continues to spit out the shells until she realizes she has already emptied the whole package. The tip of her tongue feels numb. With a sigh, she leans back on the sofa, looks at the dark shadow on the ceiling reflected from the single floor lamp beside her.

Suddenly her phone rings. A string of musical notes bounces back and forth within the walls of her small apartment, bringing her mind back from another world. Who would be calling her at this odd hour? She picks up the receiver from the corner of her desk.

"Hello?" she greets softly.

"Mei, it's me, Hua!"

Yi Mei can't believe this! They didn't talk for three years, now twice this evening. "Let me call you back, it's cheaper that way," she suggests. She still has two dollars left on her phone card. They can talk for at least another hour.

"It's OK. I just want to talk a bit more with you," Ai Hua persists.

Yi Mei senses Ai Hua must have something important to tell her.

"I think, in your mind," Ai Hua starts, "in your mind, I know, you regard me as a man." She pauses, as if searching for a proper expression. "Somehow, you treat me like a man, like a husband."

"What?" Yi Mei's mind has been totally fried. What is her friend talking about now? Is she referring to the characters in the story? Or their relationship in real life?

In Yi Mei's story about three divorced women, two characters who spend more time together seem like they could be lovers. In fact, when Yi Mei was drafting the story, at some point she thought she could make them lesbian lovers—because they had rediscovered their sexuality through mutual support and natural instinct. She knew a few women like that at work, whose failed marriages and subsequent divorces led them to question traditional wedlock. Later those female colleagues chose one another instead of male companions. But that was only a passing thought in the process of writing. In the end, Yi Mei didn't make her two divorcées lesbian. She felt it would be too radical for Chinese culture, even though her story was written in English for the readers in the west.

"Remember the last night we spent together. When you were leaning against me, I felt as if you were treating me as your husband," Ai Hua's voice interrupts Yi Mei's train of thought.

Now Yi Mei assumes Ai Hua is talking about their personal relationship rather than the characters in the story. "So did you mind?" she asks curiously.

Yi Mei can still visualize that evening; Ai Hua in a blue silk nightgown after a shower, her full breasts and pointing nipples sticking out through the soft silk. Suddenly Yi Mei was so aroused that she went up to Ai Hua and started stroking her breasts despite herself. The two old friends spent the night in Ai Hua's apartment. While they were talking about guys they had met, Ai Hua kissed Yi Mei's neck and Yi Mei caressed Ai Hua's breasts. Eventually, they fell asleep on the same pillow. The next morning nothing was said between them when Yi Mei bid goodbye.

"Mei, can you find me an old man in Canada to marry?" Ai Hua asks out of the blue; her voice sounds mischievous.

"Why?" Yi Mei is shocked by Ai Hua's request.

"Because I want to come to Canada. I want to see you, spend time with you. I don't care whether he is an old man as long as he can bring me to you in Canada; I just want to be closer to you." Ai Hua's voice is loud and voluptuous, filling up Yi Mei's tiny apartment. "I hope I am not too old to excite an old man. Since I am 'adventurous,' according to your characterization of me, I think I can adapt to Canadian life. So can you find me a willing sponsor, Mei?"

"A willing sponsor?" Yi Mei repeats, laughing loudly. "I'll put an ad in the *Toronto Star* tomorrow. It should read like this: A wanton, middle-aged Chinese woman is looking for an old, Canadian sugar daddy to marry for immigration purposes. Willing sponsor please apply with recent bank statements."

Over the phone, Ai Hua's loud laugher rolls over like a string of invisible pearls.

They hang up. What Ai Hua has said can't all be a joke—it hides a genuine desire. But what can she do in Canada? She doesn't speak much English; she doesn't drive; she is too old to be an exotic dancer, which would be the wrong category of employment for immigration any way. Didn't the prime minister recently fire the minister responsible for immigration for allowing a foreign stripper to enter Canada?

Yi Mei feels she needs some fresh air to clear her head. Putting on her down overcoat and sliding her feet inside the tall winter boots at the door, she locks up her apartment.

Outside, fresh puffy snow covers the entire street and the sidewalks. Yi Mei walks slowly, inhaling the cool air. Pulling off her gloves, she grabs a handful of snow to rub on her face. There is little traffic. Before her is a beautiful winter wonderland. Soon it will be Christmas and New Year.

A delivery person is filling up the newspaper box at the street corner.

Suddenly Yi Mei feels she wants to share her life with someone, someone who seeks love in a relationship with her, and someone she can love in return.

Is that person Ai Hua? Yi Mei asks herself.

Yi Mei hears a thunder cracking loud inside her head, breaking through the twenty-year silence in her life.

Turning around, she rushes back to her apartment, believing she must be truly mad tonight. Once inside, with her high boots and long overcoat still on, she dials Ai Hua's number.

"Mei!" Before the first ring ends, Ai Hua has picked up the phone as if she was expecting Yi Mei's call.

"Hua! It *is* me! But how do you know?"

"A woman's sixth sense," answers Ai Hua playfully.

"Listen, Hua, I can be your willing and legal sponsor according to a new law in Canada."

And she tells Ai Hua the biggest news of the year that's appeared in today's paper—the Supreme Court of Canada has recognized the constitutional rights of same-sex couples.

Water and Soil

A BOEING 777 AIRBUS CRUISES at 31,000 feet altitude towards Beijing. Shirley Zhang, sitting beside a window, glances at the small television screen in front of her. Total distance: 6660 miles, projected flying time: 13 hours and 40 minutes.

Outside the small aircraft window, the blue sky becomes more extensive and voluminous; bright sunshine bounces off the silver wing of the plane. The jet has already crossed the Arctic Ocean, the Berlin Sea, the city of Anchorage, and the International Time Zone. Shirley looks at her watch: 8 P.M. Toronto time, but according to Asian time, this is actually the morning of the next day. With each passing minute, her anxiety grows; in less than five hours, she will be landing on the soil of her birth country, her first return visit home after being away for fifteen years.

Fifteen years ago, at twenty-seven, Shirley left China for Canada to pursue her postgraduate studies. In Toronto, she developed a mysterious ailment; she couldn't stop gagging after each meal, behaving almost like a pregnant woman. Sometimes on buses or in the classroom, her roiling stomach would throw up.

One morning, in the women's washroom of Robarts Library at the University, Shirley felt sick again while bending over the sink to wash her hands.

"Morning sick?" asked a stranger, washing her hands beside Shirley.

"All-day sick," Shirley lifted up her head with a grin. "In fact, I've been sick ever since I came to Canada," she said, pointing at her stomach, as if the stranger were a doctor.

The woman asked Shirley a few questions. Drying her hands below a hand-blower on the wall, she said slowly and thoughtfully, "In Chinese medicine, this is called 'water and soil disorder'"

"What does that mean?" asked Shirley curiously.

"It means your system is distressed by the new elements in this place and is therefore temporarily disoriented."

Shirley had never met anyone who could name her stomach discomfort with such a profound and precise philosophical analysis. Looking up at the middle-aged woman dressed elegantly in a long skirt and matching jacket, Shirley said, "I definitely feel disoriented." She could still taste some bitterness even after rinsing her mouth several times. "Can Chinese medicine treat it?"

The stranger paused for a few seconds, then in almost a secretive tone, asked, "Did you, by any chance, bring a small pouch of Chinese soil to Canada?"

Shirley, feeling totally bewildered, asked, "Did you say 'soil'?"

"Yes, a small parcel of homeland soil, dug perhaps from the backyard or the garden of your home in China," the woman explained.

"Why, why would I want to bring a packet of soil from China to Canada?" Even more confused now, Shirley wanted to joke with the stranger that she was not a biologist, nor a dirt snake farmer. Soil? She laughed. She wasn't even sure the other woman was still talking about her stomach problem. Perhaps she should end this crazy conversation in the women's washroom.

"Have you never heard about traditional Chinese therapies?" The stranger persisted.

"Yes, of course. Some," Shirley responded positively, "but I never knew a remedy that uses soil."

"This one does. It needs soil. It is called Ginger Soup therapy."

The two women stepped out of the washroom. In the lobby, Shirley took out a notepad and pencil from her schoolbag. The other woman dictated to her a traditional Chinese herbal recipe:

Ginger Soup for Water and Soil Disorder
One cup of fresh, sliced ginger root;
add a tablespoon of soil from your homeland;
add two cups of water;
bring to a boil, and lower the heat;
keep boiling half an hour . . .

Shirley went to Chinatown at Spadina and Dundas Streets and bought five pounds of fresh ginger root. The cashier, weighing the heavy bag of ginger on the scale, looked somewhat amused. A reflective smile appeared on her face before she asked Shirley, "Are you planning to make vinegar ginger?"

"What?"

Shirley had picked up a bottle of rice vinegar as well.

"Don't you know vinegar ginger cures diarrhea caused by 'water and soil disorder'?" asked the cashier compassionately.

Shirley couldn't believe this! A second ginger remedy offered by a local Chinese. Water and soil disorder must be a common problem suffered by newcomers. Both strangers sounded like the barefoot doctors she had met during the Chinese Cultural Revolution in the seventies. Those self-taught, grass-roots medical personnel applied acupuncture and herbal remedies to treat common ailments, especially in the countryside. But now in Canada, how could she accept these unsophisticated recipes as medical advice?

That evening Shirley stuffed an empty jar with slices of ginger root and poured in half the bottle of Chinese vinegar. She remembered an old Chinese saying, "Treat a dead horse as if it were still alive," meaning you had nothing to lose when you were desperately looking for a cure. She also decided to make a pot of ginger soup by modifying the original ginger soup recipe. Without homeland soil, she used the soil she had dug out from behind Robarts Library. She even dripped some maple syrup into the soup in place of brown sugar. She thought about her modifications carefully. Shouldn't she start absorbing Canadian elements into her system? Why didn't she adapt to Canadian soil instead of lingering over the homeland soil that was thousands of miles away? Her modification of the original recipe seemed to make a lot of sense and somehow she thought it might just work.

It turned out that her homemade ginger soup tasted quite all right to her sensitive palate; the pungent ginger was softened by the dark Canadian soil and sweetened by the maple syrup. She gulped it down three, four times a day, feeling like a new-age warrior, using a natural remedy to cure an unknown ailment.

She was delighted when, after a month, her system miraculously relocated itself to Canadian soil.

The lights in the cabin are switched on. Two airline attendants push a tall stainless steel cart down the aisle. It's time for morning refreshments. The airline's lukewarm coffee, handed over politely by the steward, makes her frown. At home, she looks forward to making her morning coffee; she doesn't even buy ground coffee. Instead, she keeps a small bag of medium-roast Colombia coffee beans in the freezer. Every morning, she grinds two full tablespoons of coffee beans in a small wooden hand-grinder. Then she puts the freshly ground coffee in a small filter; meanwhile the kettle is boiling. She pours steaming hot water slowly into the filter. While the aroma of fresh coffee fills up her kitchen, she turns on her radio for CBC morning news and music. Shirley remembers her friends commenting on how well she has blended into western culture; some even predicted that she might experience reverse culture shock on her first trip home after being away for fifteen years. Now she swallows the lukewarm coffee, thinking about how to readapt herself to Chinese customs and habits.

Shortly after serving the beverages, the airline attendants come back with boxed instant noodle soup. Shirley suddenly feels nostalgic. Instant noodle soup used to be the most popular snack in the students' dormitory in China in the 1980s. She can still visualize her classmates sitting on the edge of their double-bunk beds, slurping noodle soup after returning from night studies.

Now sitting in the jumbo airplane, she is amazed to see how her fellow passengers skillfully lift up the paper lids of their soup cups. An attendant walks by with a kettle and pours hot water into each cup and closes down the lid. Across the cabin, passengers start splitting apart their disposable bamboo chopsticks—which are fused together at one end—making tiny, audible, snapping sounds. A few minutes later, Shirley hears sounds of slurping here and there. She turns to look at who is making the unbecoming sounds. No one seems as alarmed as she is. Shirley wonders whether slurping is okay in the west now; after all, instant noodle soup has already crossed the International Time Zone. The truth is, how can anyone eat noodle soup any other way? Her fellow passengers are engaged in different activities, some listening to jazz or classical music, others reading *America Today*, *Business News*, and *Vogue*. Their hands are busy as their minds are preoccupied; most of them use one hand to hold the soup cup close to their lips. And the only efficient way to get the noodles into the mouth is naturally by slurping.

Shirley smiles, wondering what her old teacher, James, would say if he were here to witness the passengers slurping in the plane. She can't help laughing at her own thought, because it was James who taught her how to have soup with a spoon without making any sound.

"Scoop up the soup with your spoon and lift it up to your mouth," James, his right arm hanging in the air, demonstrated the western soup-eating technique in a series of slow motions. Shirley, his student from China, was sitting at the dinner table, her eyes wide open.

"Once inside your mouth, turn the spoon sideways, or upside down. The key part is not to suck the soup before it gets inside your mouth. When the soup is inside your mouth, swallow it quietly.

Sucking makes a slurping noise. In the west, it is very rude to eat noisily at the table."

James finished his demonstration.

There was a bowl of soup before each of them. It was French soup made with broccoli, garlic, potato, and milk and light green in colour; its texture was thick like baby food or cooked vegetables pureed for a toothless senior. Shirley hesitated with her spoon, thinking about the difference between "drink soup" in Chinese and "have soup" in English—neither was accurate enough to describe what they were doing. She looked at her teacher, who was in the process of swallowing a spoonful of soup. Shirley quietly switched the topic.

"How do you show appreciation?"

"Oh, that's easy, Shirley, you should know the answer." James looked quite surprised at his student from China, and after a long pause, continued, "You just say thank you."

"But a thank-you sounds so plain. It simply can't express how much you have enjoyed the delicious soup and how grateful you are to your host or hostess for making it."

James listened to Shirley attentively, his spoon resting on the edge of the bowl. "Let's see, you want to praise the soup. You can always use some descriptive adjectives, such as delicious, tasteful, delicate, great flavour, and so on."

"Words, words, words," Shirley laughed. "You stop eating to search for synonyms in a thesaurus."

Having lived in Canada for fifteen years, Shirley has her soup silently now. In fact, she would be alarmed, as she is now, if someone had soup noisily.

James, Shirley murmurs, you won in the end.

But right now, why not use slurping as a means to getting back to the Chinese way? It has just dawned on Shirley that she might be able to avoid reverse culture shock if she starts to behave like a Chinese in China during the flight. By the time the plane lands, she might feel like a fish going back to the water.

Anyway, sooner or later the rest of the world will have to adopt some Chinese manners anyway, since China now supplies the whole world with cheap products.

Hey, James, did you ever experience water and soil disorder when you first landed in China to teach us? Ever since boarding this flight, Shirley can't stop chatting to James in her head.

When Shirley was a fourth-year English major, her university hired two Americans and one Canadian to teach courses in the English department. Those foreigners were pioneers who were friendly towards China and curious about its culture. James was on his sabbatical leave from a Canadian college that year. Besides teaching English, he also wanted to investigate what he believed was a better political system in China.

"Why are you so keen on studying abroad?" James was puzzled by his students' many questions regarding how to apply to Canadian and American universities. He explained to them in great detail that education could be unbelievably expensive for foreign students in North America. But to his surprise, he couldn't discourage his Chinese students from wanting to pursue their dreams abroad. In the end, James could only blame the United States of America for spreading its poisonous Coca-Cola and its doomed materialistic ways to the rest of the world.

"Don't you know that capitalism is based on the rich exploiting the poor?" James voiced the question repeatedly. "The Chinese system, by and large, is a much better one. In China, everybody has a job. Men and women enjoy equal pay for doing the same work." He couldn't believe that he, a Canadian, a foreigner, voluntarily stood up to defend the Chinese system to the Chinese. Wasn't this a typical example of irony, a rhetorical device that he was teaching his students?

Shirley and her classmates had some heated debates with James. They criticized his logic as contradictory. Shirley told him that on one hand, he wanted to help China develop its education, but on the other, he would rather China stay a Third World country. However, the Chinese people didn't want to belong to the underdeveloped world forever. As long as they remained poor, western people would always enjoy superiority over the Chinese. And this privilege of the west would only perpetuate the historical inequality between East and West. The reason that she, her classmates, and thousands of other Chinese students wanted to study abroad was that they were as curious about the Western world as he was about China, and they had never been allowed to think about studying abroad before.

A year after Shirley came to Canada, James retired from his job at a community college in Toronto. A few months later, he invited Shirley to meet him at the Copenhagen Room, a famous Danish restaurant on St Thomas Street, just south of Bloor and west of Yonge Street.

"I am going to China tomorrow," James said, startling Shirley as soon as they sat down at a corner table.

"What? Are you joking?" Shirley burst out.

"No, I am not," answered James seriously. "I am going to teach English at Kunming University in southwestern China for a year. But for some strange reason, at this last moment, I am not sure whether I should be going." James looked at Shirley, his eyes clouded by a rarely seen uncertainty.

"Maybe you shouldn't be going." Shirley felt that James should not be in such a rush to go to China.

"But I think it might be too late for me to change the decision. First of all, I can't cancel my flight for tomorrow morning," James sighed, raising a small glass of whiskey. "So I came to say goodbye to you."

Shirley knew James loved China tremendously and that he wouldn't turn down a teaching position, especially when he was no longer working in Canada. But why did he wait so long before breaking the news to his friends? Obviously, he didn't want anyone to interfere with his decision. As it turned out now, it would be too late for him to change his plans.

In James's dreamy eyes, Shirley saw the reflection of the bronze statue of a little mermaid sitting at the entrance. Shirley sensed why

James, perhaps subconsciously, chose their last meeting place at the Copenhagen Room. She seemed to see a connection with the little mermaid. After his retirement, James probably felt like a small boat being tossed by waves in the ocean without a clear direction, and he couldn't refuse a job offer from China just as the sailors couldn't resist the mermaid's sweet, homecoming song from a distant harbour. From now on, James would charge up his boat and sail towards his destiny.

"Shirley, do you know that according to statistics, more Canadians die in their bathtubs at home each year than in adventures abroad?" James laughed and drank up his whiskey. With a gesture, he brushed off her concern and his own momentary uncertainty.

And so James left for Kunming University in China. Three months later, Shirley received a short letter from him, saying he was looking forward to his reunion with his old students in Wuhan during the winter vacation and the Chinese New Year. Back in Toronto, Shirley imagined her classmates coming back to the university during the holidays to be reunited with their beloved Canadian professor.

Three weeks later, on an icy cold wintry night, news came that James had died in Wuhan suddenly, the night before he was scheduled to leave for Beijing.

Shirley rushed out of her room. Braving the cold sidewalks, she ran all the way to James's favourite restaurant, the Copenhagen Room, as if he were waiting for her there. She wanted to get drunk on whiskey to release her unbearable pain. Why hadn't she persuaded him to cancel his trip that day? She blamed herself. When she got to the restaurant's location, she found out that it had closed permanently for quite some time.

Shirley collapsed on the icy cold marble stairs at the entrance, her hands grabbing the dust-covered wooden railings, and she cried in the darkness.

Where was the little mermaid?

The night before his departure for Beijing, James had a busy schedule.

First, he went to visit Shirley's parents and had *Jiaozi*, dumplings, with her family. After that he met with two groups of his old students. He had several glasses of *Mao Tai*, the Chinese whiskey, and some steamed *juicy baozi* at the famous Four Seasons Restaurant in Wuhan. It was after midnight when he finally returned to the university guest house. He decided to take a bath before going to bed. He died in the bathtub, possibly of a stroke.

James's death shocked the university campus. Because he was Canadian, a foreigner, the city's Security Bureau and the Foreign Affairs Department organized a joint investigation. All those involved with James on his last day were called in one after another for an interview with the public security officers. They were told to write down all the details about what had happened during their meeting with James. Shirley's family was also interviewed. The officer came home and wrote a three-page statement detailing the dinner the family had with James. He started from the moment the Canadian professor stepped into the apartment with his interpreter to the time the family waved goodbye as the taxi was pulling out. His statement also included a conversation between James and Shirley's five-year-old niece:

"Does *jiaozi* grow on top of trees?" James teased the little girl. "I want to plant some *jiaozi* trees in Canada."

"No," the little girl giggled, "you can't grow *jiaozi*. My grandmother made them. She rolled the dough first, and made a ball with minced pork and vegetables."

A week after Shirley's return to her home city, she is as busy as a spinning top. Friends and relatives take turns to invite her out for lunch and dinner. She finally has the chance to enjoy the delicious local specialties, in particular the famous hot-and-dry noodles and the deep-fried, unsweetened, rice donuts that were her childhood favorites. She slurps along with the folks when she drinks tea or eats noodles. At the end of each meal, she thanks the hosts for their hospitality, since local custom forbids guests to share the expenses.

In return, Shirley invites her friends to visit her in Canada in the future when Chinese people can travel freely like Europeans and North Americans. Her friends give her the polite Chinese smile. Shirley knows most of them think that will never happen, that she is only paying lip service.

Shirley expected she would be like a fish returning to the sea where she belonged, but so far this hasn't happened. All the welcome-back gatherings have further widened the fifteen-years' gap of her absence from home. She walks around with a city map in her hands, which reminds her of her true identity as a stranger, a foreigner in China.

The streets have extended in all directions, from the place she used to call home to the suburbs. Expressways above the streets make her feel dizzy and disoriented. By the end of the week, Shirley has a strange feeling that perhaps she hasn't yet conquered her jetlag. Otherwise, why is she feeling so dislocated?

On Monday Shirley is invited by her university to have lunch with her classmates and teachers, who are now professors. For convenience, they tell her to take a taxi, because it is too complicated for a stranger to get around by public transportation.

A twenty-minute taxi ride takes her from her parents' apartment building to her former university. The vehicle turns inside the gate and stops at the security post.

Shirley asks the driver, "Where is the cabbage field that used to be in front of the university?"

"What cabbage?" the driver laughs, pointing at the security guard. "Ask him."

Looking around a full circle, Shirley doesn't see a single cabbage, or cowboy, or cow girl, or even a water buffalo. New buildings, to use a Chinese saying, have risen up like young bamboo shoots after a spring shower. From deep inside the campus, Shirley hears high-pitched whistles and the dull noise of a cement mixer.

"James, where are you?" Shirley yells towards the campus. "I am home!"

Sitting at the head of the table at lunch is Shirley's former teacher, now the President of the Foreign Language Institute. A dozen cold and hot dishes garnished with decorative carved vegetables make this reception a special one for the returning graduate. The hosts and the guest talk about the changes on campus with nostalgic memories of the old days. The lunch lasts about an hour. Two of Shirley's classmates, Xiao Wang and Xiao Zhang, volunteer to show her around.

Once outside the Guest House, Shirley anxiously asks them about James's funeral.

"The week after James passed away, the campus was draped in black and white cloth in deep mourning," Xiao Wang recalls.

"The students he had taught came from all over the province to say goodbye," Xiao Zhang adds.

"Do you remember his old-fashioned, Mao-style jacket with four pockets at the front?" Xiao Wang asks Shirley.

"Of course, I do," Shirley nods with a smile. They all still remember the first day when James wore the jacket to class.

"Lying in the coffin in his favourite navy blue Chinese jacket, James looked truly peaceful," Xiao Wang continues, "as if he had chosen the right place to die."

"His body was cremated and some of the ashes were buried on campus."

Shirley's eyes feel wet. "Can you take me there?" she begs.

Her two classmates stare at each other for a second, and then look down at their feet.

"I would like to see where his ashes are buried," Shirley repeats, wondering whether she has made herself understood.

To her surprise, neither of the women know where the burial ground is.

"I heard there is a red maple planted on top of the burial site to mark the spot," Shirley reminds them.

Shirley had thought there would be an annual remembrance ceremony for James. But . . . have they already forgotten about him?

The two former classmates apologize to Shirley. Xiao Zhang offers to call the central office on her cellphone.

The secretary on duty says that before the construction crew broke the ground for the new administration building, the English Department was told to remove James's ashes. But where did they move the pot of ashes to? She has no idea. Nobody in her office seems to know either, the secretary says, especially now that it is summer.

The two classmates look at each other like guilty parties in front of a judge.

"But James loved us!" Shirley pleads. "This Canadian loved his Chinese students and their university to the last minute of his life!"

The women invite Shirley back to the guest house. They promise her that they will do their best to locate James. They won't disappoint her because she came all the way from Canada. They just need to make a few more phone calls.

After half an hour or so, her classmates come back with the good news. Xiao Wang excitedly tells Shirley that they have found the only person on campus who actually knows about the removal of James's ashes.

Shirley lets out a deep sigh of relief.

That person turns out to be one of Shirley's classmates from a different year, a quiet, reticent fellow originally from the countryside. Xiao Yang used to sit in the last row of the class. After graduation, he worked as a librarian for the English Department. Recently he has been promoted as the Master of the Foreign Affairs Institute in the university.

Turning Shirley over to Master Yang, the two women say their goodbyes. Shirley follows Master Yang towards a different direction on campus.

"I moved James myself," Master Yang recalls. "He was literally only a few centimetres away from where the claw of a giant CAT was about to dig up the whole lot." A faint smile appears at the corners of his dry lips.

Shirley holds her breath; she imagines Master Yang running towards the construction site, heroically jumping into the pit, just like in a movie. He digs out the jar of ashes with his bare hands.

"And since the university didn't provide me with another lot, I have secretly buried him under a shrub." Master Yang stops in front of a raised flower box, a square wooden structure made from retired railway sleepers.

In this tiny flowerbed, and underneath a nameless low shrub, whose branches and leaves are dusted with construction debris, lie the ashes of their beloved teacher, James, the Chinese people's great friend from Canada.

As a Canadian, Shirley is proud of James, who dedicated his life to his friendship with the Chinese people. In her mind, James is as great as that other famous Canadian in China, Dr Norman Bethune, who also gave his life to China. Chairman Mao once wrote an article to commemorate Dr Bethune's internationalism. And this article was read by millions of Chinese every day during the Cultural Revolution. Shirley wants to cry, thinking this is how the traditionally hospitable Chinese treat one of their best friends now. She will wail so loudly that she hopes to wake up the dead.

Master Yang moves closer to the shrub, as if looking for something, his hands brushing the branches and leaves. "Here, here it is!" he cries out happily. "I know I remember exactly where it is! Look at this, the original plaque."

Shirley steps forward stiffly, her limbs feeling numb. With her index finger, she gently wipes off the dust from a piece of wood hanging on a branch. The oval-shaped plaque is no bigger than the size of her palm. It was originally painted navy blue; some faint words written in light yellow paint are barely visible. She recognizes James's full name, his birthday, and the day he passed away. Exchanging a quick look with Master Yang, Shirley lowers her head. She tells herself that this is the exact spot that she has been looking for! She must believe that James was buried here, right here!

Shirley feels her head is about to explode. Her limbs feel numb as she stands there like a bronze statue, completely at one with the ground under her feet.

After a long time, Shirley asks Master Yang, "What happened to the red maple?"

"Unfortunately, the red maple didn't survive. I removed it the same day to this flowerbed, but it didn't make it. Perhaps it suffered from a water and soil disorder," says Master Yang regrettably.

"There, James, that's for you, an example of irony and black humour from your best students," Shirley murmurs, tasting the salty tears running down her cheeks, her hands patting the branches of the shrub as if consoling an old friend.

Opening her knapsack, Shirley takes out a small plastic bag and a water bottle carefully tied up with rubber band. First, she unties the plastic bag, from which she carefully releases upon the base of the shrub some black soil she has dug from behind Robarts Library on St George Street in Toronto. Then she flips open the water bottle and slowly pours the water from Lake Ontario onto the soil.

Neighbours

BATHED IN THE BRIGHT early summer sunshine, Sally stands at the northeastern side of Yonge Street and Eglinton Avenue, waiting for the traffic lights to change. She has recently moved to the area because it's one of Toronto's more vibrant neighbourhoods. The two streets at the intersection are not wide; when the traffic lights switch to red for either of the streets, for a moment the entire block is put on hold, as it were. Drivers rest their feet on the brakes; pedestrians at the four corners have an opportunity to exchange looks. Sally knows this happens at all the intersections of the city, and standing elbow to elbow among strangers reminds her of Beijing, the city where she lived for thirty years before coming to Canada. Sally likes the big city, where she can be close to excitement and at the same time not be involved if she doesn't want to. She can be an onlooker, like right now at the street corner, waiting for the traffic lights to switch.

Sally holds a Styrofoam coffee cup in her hand as she listens to the rhythm of morning traffic. Calculating the time she has before the lights change, she tips over the cup carefully to her lips, so that it doesn't spill over her new silk jacket. Walking toward a garbage stand, and using the empty coffee cup to pop open the flapping device, she tries to drop the cup in without getting her fingers dirty. But for some bizarre reason, the white cup falls onto the sidewalk and rolls away

79

like a wheel. Sally is annoyed. Now her traffic light has turned green, opening a floodgate, and pedestrians rush into the street. Intuitively, Sally follows. Half way across, she turns around. Did she forget something?

Sally sees a thin old man bending down on the sidewalks near the garbage stand. His head is below her eye level, so she can't see his face, but the top of his head has thin brown hair. His bony shoulders stretching forward and one hand resting on his knee for support, with his other hand he picks up the Styrofoam cup from the sidewalk. Sally's face turns red. Why didn't she take care of her own responsibility? But now in the middle of the crossing, she doesn't have time to ponder over her guilt. The traffic lights in front of her are turning amber, she hurries over to the south side of Eglinton and then into the subway.

Sometimes when she stands at the intersection of Yonge and Eglinton, waiting for the traffic lights to change, Sally wonders why there are more newspaper boxes than trees in the area. Does this mean people in this neighbourhood read more? It seems that way. She has just discovered a Toronto Public Library branch north of Eglinton. She remembers that in the public libraries in China, readers were not allowed inside the book stacks area, the librarians would go in to fetch the books. To her surprise, here readers of all ages and from all walks of life go through the bookshelves themselves. Sally can find up-to-date academic magazines and various government documents for her research projects. The library has ample space too. When she gets tired, she can browse through fashion and art magazines or go upstairs to view an art exhibition. She watches kids flipping through books with such intense interest that they remind her of her own daughter left temporarily behind in China. If only she could bring her here now! How much the six-year-old would enjoy the books!

Through the loudspeakers comes an announcement that the library is closing in ten minutes. Sally gathers her notes from the table. Stretching her back with a silent yawn she feels her left foot touch something rolling on the floor. She looks down, it's an empty Coke can. Two teenage boys shared the table with her this evening. It must have been left by them, though drinking is not allowed inside the library. Teenagers all over the world are the same! The overhead lights start to blink as a reminder. From the nearby tables several readers get up to leave. Sally puts her notes inside her folder. People walk by her table on both sides. Suddenly, from the corner of an eye she sees a man bend down to pick up something near her feet. Oh, the empty Coke can! She feels embarrassed as if she were the guilty party. "It's not me, I didn't drink here," she stammers to explain.

"I didn't say it's you, Miss," answers the man politely. "I just don't like to see people litter, that's all." The man didn't blame her; she feels relieved. But why didn't she pick it up earlier when she touched it with her foot?

Heading towards the red exit sign, Sally recalls the incident of the old man picking up her coffee cup from the sidewalk a few weeks before. Is it the same man? No, it can't be. Today the guy is in his forties and he has full black hair. It's not the same man. Then there is something about Canadians, she mumbles to herself, they care about their environment. At the exit, she watches the man drop the empty coke can and a clear water bottle into a plastic blue box.

Down Yonge Street the scent of fresh lilacs brushes her face like a soft breeze. An old couple sits on a bench in Eglinton Square, a cane leaning beside the woman. What are old people doing here at night? Watching the traffic lights? Sally recalls a similar scene in Beijing. One afternoon, she was at the Xidan Book City, one of Beijing's most popular stores. There were a lot of people outside on the square, some sat around the base of its outdoor sculpture, which depicted a pile of huge books. Sally decided to rest her feet, so she sat down next to an old couple who had several shopping bags. Suddenly, the old man stood up, passing his plastic bags to the woman, and ran towards the sidewalk. He shoved one arm inside a public garbage stand, from which he pulled out an empty water bottle. Sally was bewildered. The old man walked back to the woman, looking triumphant as if he had a trophy in his hand. "Are you—collecting bottles?" Sally saw that inside the bags on the old woman's lap were empty soft drink cans and water bottles. "What for?"

"Sell them," said the old woman, as her husband put the empty water bottle inside a shopping bag.

"How much can you get?" Sally asked, curiously.

"Ten cents each," he answered humbly, "not much, but it helps. We're old, factory closed down, no pension." He sighed.

The old woman passed a wet towel to her husband. "Clean your hands." She turned around to Sally and said, "You see, young lady, if we can each pick up a hundred bottles or cans every day, we make 20 *yuan* a day. That's 600 *yuan* a month, and we can live on that."

"Good for the environment," Sally murmured, knowing that the old couple didn't need her moral analysis. At the time, she didn't know the word "recycling."

But now she knows the word and appreciates the concept. But going out of the way to pick up other people's litter as these Canadians do is beyond her. Passing the old couple sitting in Eglinton Square, Sally has a naughty thought: if she dares to drop an empty Coke can on the sidewalk, she can bet on getting a public flogging by the old woman with her cane!

Warm summer breeze soon changes young lemon-green leaves to dark foliage. Flowers of many kinds and colours bloom in front of restaurants and stores. Then comes Canada Day! Sally is not a Canadian, but she hopes one day she will be, because she has begun to like this country and its people. A notice on the library's bulletin board says that on Canada Day there will be an outdoor concert in Eglinton Square. So here comes Sally, wearing a cool white cotton dress with red birds flying, their wings spread out wide. The colours of Canada Day. In front of the Grand and Toy store there is a crowd. Rows of chairs in the sun, some seats still waiting occupancy. Three wheelchairs are parked in the back. Sitting down, Sally smiles at the old couple next to her.

"I'm Elizabeth, and this is my husband, Joe," smiles the old woman. "Go get yourself a free drink, Miss." Elizabeth motions towards the front.

"Don't be shy," adds Joe encouragingly.

Sally feels inadequate; but after watching others drinking from identical plastic cups, she goes up to the front and picks up a cup of ginger ale on the table. The Salvation Army Band is here: middle-aged and senior men and women dressed in out-of-date uniforms, looking both funny and serious. They play a good selection of music that seems to resonate around the entire neighbourhood. "Do you want to come to our building tonight? We can watch fireworks on the roof," Elizabeth says to Sally at the end of the concert.

After dinner Sally rings the buzzer to the old couple's apartment. She doesn't know exactly why she has come to visit them, strangers she has met only today. Perhaps they remind her of her own parents in China, or the old couple she met in Beijing who collected empty bottles and tin cans for a living, or perhaps it's because she wants to buy a vacuum cleaner and she needs advice. The buzzer rings like the hoarse voice of an old man. Then from the speaker comes out a woman's soft voice. "Is that Sally?"

"Yes, Elizabeth, it's me," she answers delightedly.

"Come up, 903." The door hisses, opens slowly.

Inside the one-bedroom apartment, Sally feels disoriented, thinks perhaps she's having an illusion that she is inside a country farmhouse. The furniture is old and heavy with carvings on the back of the chairs and on the legs of the table. It reminds her of the furniture her family owned before the Cultural Revolution. Later the Red Guards threw it into a bonfire. On the walls, there are framed photos in light brown or dark gray. There is a large balcony outside the sitting room, but from where she stands, Sally thinks it looks like a workshop.

Joe tells Sally to make herself at home, Elizabeth offers a choice of tea or coffee. "Because I was born on April 21 and have the same birthday as the Queen, my parents named me after her," she smiles, "but my husband is not Philip, Duke of Edinburgh, you know, what's his last name?" She laughs. "So, would you like to have a cup of English tea?"

"I'd love to have a cup of English tea, Madam," Sally puts on a mock British accent. They all laugh.

Over a cup of Red Rose tea, Sally takes out the latest flyer from Future Shop, the store a few blocks north. She asks the couple what kind of vacuum cleaner is more effective and less expensive.

Putting on his reading glasses, Joe starts reading the advertisement. He mumbles and grumbles to himself, shaking his head. "Too expensive, too much money," he continues to shake his head as he speaks.

"That's what I think," echoes Sally, "but we can do nothing about their prices."

"Yes, of course you can." Joe puts down the ad on the coffee table.

"Like what?" Sally asks suspiciously.

"If you don't mind a refurbished model, I have one for you," says Joe.

Sally doesn't understand the word "refurbished," but she understands the second part of the sentence. Joe has a vacuum cleaner for her. Is he a salesperson? Her eyes quickly sweep over his face. She cautions herself that she shouldn't buy anything before first doing her own research. Meanwhile Joe has stepped out onto the balcony. Shortly he brings in a red vacuum cleaner. "Here it is, refurbished, this baby is like new," he beams at Sally and Elizabeth, patting the body of the vacuum cleaner affectionately. Plugging it into a power outlet, Joe rolls the roaring machine on the floor like a dancer.

Sally doesn't know what to say. After Joe has turned the appliance on and off and returned to the sofa to finish his tea, she asks him timidly, "So, how much is it?" She had no idea that this old man, a neighbour she met this morning, sells secondhand vacuum cleaners in his apartment.

"Two hundred dollars, no taxes," Joe says seriously. Then he bursts out laughing. "A real deal, young lady."

"No, Joe, please don't joke with her," his wife interrupts.

"OK." Joe stops laughing. "Sally, didn't I make myself understood? You can *have* it, I mean, have it, take it home, if you don't mind a refurbished model."

"It's yours if you need it," Elizabeth repeats.

"Really, free for me?" Sally asks, not quite believing. "Thank you very much, I would be delighted to take it home. But what are you going to use?"

"Oh, don't worry, we have our own. You see, Joe picks up stuff from the dump behind the building," Elizabeth says, "you know, residents throw things away, when they are not working."

"But a lot of the times, there is nothing seriously wrong with the machines," Joe says, raising his voice to emphasize. "It's just dust, dirt, you know. People dispose of just about anything nowadays." He starts to shake his head again. His wife nods.

"So you repair them?" Sally can figure out what happens next.

"Yes, he spends time cleaning them up and making them work again," Elizabeth says. "Then he gives them away to people who need them. Over there, on the balcony, go have a look."

Getting up from the sofa, Joe motions to her. "Come, come with me, I'll show you."

Sally follows him.

This is not exactly what a balcony is supposed to be, Sally thinks. It's a workshop. A large toolbox, a working bench, and a tabletop. On the shelves, built against one of the walls, Sally recognizes various objects: a manual sewing machine, a coffee grinder, a food processor, an electrical wok, a few bicycle wheels and inner tires.

"All the appliances here are refurbished and in good working condition," says Joe proudly. Sally smiles, her vocabulary has been enriched today with a new word, "refurbished"; she doesn't even have to look it up in a dictionary.

When they hear the noise of fireworks, Joe, Elizabeth, and Sally rush to the elevator and up onto the rooftop. Under the starry summer night sky, a cool breeze clarifies Sally's mind. Young children and teenagers have brought their music, drinks, laughter, and noise to the rooftop. Young mothers scream at their kids every now and then. Suddenly, fireworks shoot up in the distant sky; everybody exclaims.

Sally asks Joe and Elizabeth why they chose to live in a mixed building instead of one for seniors. "Wouldn't that be quieter?"

"Oh yes, it would be," Elizabeth answers, "but Joe and I like to live where things are happening, we like excitement."

"So do I," says Sally, feeling closer to the old couple than before.

"However, having said that," Joe inserts, "there are problems. In the last few years, some single mothers have moved into the building with their kids. What do kids do, eh? So, now you see graffiti inside the elevator and laundry room, you see empty pop cans in the common areas."

"We pick them up, wherever we see them," Elizabeth says.

"But what about their mothers?" Joe adds. "Do they know it's their responsibility to educate their kids? Especially, some of them don't even go to work, they live on welfare. On taxpayers' money." Joe hasn't stopped shaking his head. Sally regrets having started the topic. Now their conversation is heading towards a dead end.

Another splash of fireworks in the sky. Another interval. Sally decides to take a chance. "So, I guess you won't like me either," she looks at Joe and Elizabeth anxiously.

They don't understand. "Why? What makes you say that?" They look puzzled.

"Because, because I'm divorced and I'm a single mother," Sally says quietly. "But I'm not on welfare. Back at home, I had wished that the state had some welfare schemes to help single mothers with kids. And there weren't any. I went through a very difficult period after my divorce. Sometimes, in order to save money for food, I walked three hours to get home instead of taking a bus." Sally doesn't know why she tells this to the old couple. It's not relevant. This is Canada. People here don't understand it. But for some reason she wants to share her experiences with them, wants them to understand. So she continues,

"Perhaps the single mothers in your building have circumstances you don't know about. Perhaps they are struggling against their personal crises. Perhaps they need advice, just as I did with the vacuum cleaner."

In the open sky there goes the loudest explosion of the night. Hundreds of rockets shooting up and exploding, tens and thousands of colourful flowers flashing and glittering in the sky. Sally, Joe and Elizabeth clap their hands like kids.

It's around midnight when Sally bids good night. Joe and Elizabeth give her big hugs and kisses on the cheeks. They would like to have her over for dinner soon.

Sally walks down Yonge Street carrying the refurbished red vacuum cleaner in her hands. At the intersection, waiting for the traffic lights to change, she recognizes familiar faces from the neighbourhood. Tall Kelly is at the northwest corner, selling *Outreach*, a newspaper sold by the unemployed and the homeless. At the southeast corner, disabled George, a self-proclaimed Hollywood agent, sits on the granite steps outside the CIBC branch. George usually asks people who pass by if they want to go to Hollywood. On the southwest corner, Dave's hotdog cart is still surrounded by a large crowd. Sally smiles broadly at her neighbours.

The Cactus

A TALL MAN BENDS over the open door of a taxi. After talking to the woman in the passenger seat, he gently closes the door, motioning the driver to take off. The woman, whose hands are both occupied, can't wave back at the old man except to look at him with her lingering eyes and a grin on her face. After the taxi rolls away from the curb, the old man straightens up and limps along towards the entrance of the apartment building.

Above the street floats the smell of car engines mixed with that of sweet summer blossoms. The taxi merges into the evening traffic. Sitting on the passenger seat stiffly, Judy Yang is holding a bundle of old rags roughly wrapped up with scotch tape. Her hands haven't moved at all since first sitting in the taxi when the old man placed the tall bundle on her lap.

The taxi stops at the intersection; the driver throws a curious look over the back of his seat. "What is it that you are holding?" he asks the passenger.

"Cactus," answers Judy.

"Ha! I thought it was a baby, or a Royal porcelain doll."

He laughs. As a taxi driver he meets many kinds of people, but he hasn't seen anyone cuddle a cactus before.

"It means no less to my friend Mark," answers Judy seriously. "This

89

cactus has been his baby and his Royal porcelain doll for fifty years." The cactus is as old as she is.

Suddenly the taxi leaps forward, and Judy's body lurches back, but she holds on to the bundle steadily.

Six weeks ago, when the leaves were a delicate lemon green on wintry branches, Mark had called Judy. "I have some important news to tell you. After living in Canada for fifty-five years, and flying back and forth across the Atlantic Ocean over a hundred times," he paused, "I have booked my last one-way flight back to Prague."

"You did?" Judy didn't sound too surprised, having known Mark for more than two decades, ever since she first came to Canada. The old man's decision would be final.

"I have informed the building manager of my departure, sold the furniture, and made arrangements for all household items, except one. I wonder if you could take care of her."

Mark waited for Judy to comprehend his request.

Anyone overhearing the conversation would have thought that Mark had a pet that needed a loving home, but Judy knew right away that her friend was talking about the cactus he had brought to Canada from Colorado five decades ago. Having watered his plants many times while Mark was away in Europe, she knows his favourite plant quite well. This cactus is about two and half feet tall; its green column is covered with inch-long brown needles all the way up to the top.

"Sure," answered Judy firmly and without hesitation.

Mark's bedroom is on the twenty-eighth floor overlooking the park at Davisville and Mount Pleasant; Judy lives in a three-storey townhouse at the east end of Toronto on busy Danforth Avenue. When they were planning the move, Mark asked her to bring several old bath towels. "And remember, do not drive that day. I'll pay a taxi for you to take her home."

"For goodness sake, it's only a cactus," Judy complained. But realizing this might be the last time she would have to please her old chum, she swallowed the rest of her words.

Now sitting in the back seat with the cactus on her lap, Judy understands why Mark insisted she should take a taxi home. He didn't want her to leave the cactus inside the trunk of her car or on the floor. Instead, he wanted her to hold it with both hands. "She is too tall to stand on the floor; her roots will snap if the car jerks," he warned her before closing the taxi door.

Back at her house, Judy carries the tall cactus to the kitchen on the second floor. Sunshine floods in through the sliding glass doors and the window; her kitchen looks like a sunroom. She removes a pot of African violets from the top tier of the flower stand in order to give the cactus the spot right below the window. "I hope you will be happy here—though it's not as bright as Mark's place, it is the best spot in the entire house."

Judy considers herself blessed with a green thumb; whatever she plants, grows and blooms. This is still early June, on the small balcony outside the sliding kitchen doors, pansies flaunt their colourful faces like butterflies; geraniums are blooming with large balls of red flowers; rose stems are studded with yellow buds; even the wild mint that she transplanted from the French River in northern Ontario years ago has produced enough new leaves for a pot of mint tea. Inside her kitchen, violets, Buddha's beads, lucky bamboo, and other green tropical plants thrive. Mark's tall cactus is well nested among them. Its height and prickly surface create a contrasting texture. Judy smiles, satisfied that her old friend's last and only wish, before leaving Toronto for good, has been properly attended to.

It has been twenty years since Judy met Mark and his friend Pierre. That was the day that Judy stepped into a pair of new skates at a downtown skating rink near Ryerson Polytech. She hobbled along the artificial man-made rocks at the edge of the circular ice rink; gingerly she moved forward like a toddler learning to take its first step. Two middle-aged men were gliding on ice like a pair of dragonflies skimming over a lily pond; their long legs drew elegant circles, making smooth and almost musical patterns on the ice. Judy watched them enviously, while her hands held the cold cement block tightly like a rock climber hanging over a cliff.

Later that afternoon Judy was having a cup of hot chocolate in a café not too far from the rink; the door opened and in came the two men from the skating rink. They sat down at a table opposite hers. Almost simultaneously, each pulled out a monocle from an inside pocket and fitted it over an eye. Judy burst out laughing, nearly choking on her hot chocolate. The two gentlemen looked like characters from a nineteenth century novel. They couldn't possibly be the same men who were flying over the rink an hour ago. Hearing her laughter, the men turned around, intuitively pulling the strings of the monocles off their eyes, which only made Judy laugh some more. This time some hot chocolate went down her windpipe, and she coughed loudly.

The men looked concerned. "Are you all right, lady skater?"

"Mm-mm, fine, I am fine," Judy answered, putting a hand over her mouth.

"What's so funny?" one of them asked. "You must let us share it."

"Mm, actually, you two, I wish I had a camera," answered Judy, suppressing a laugh.

The two men exchanged a few words in French, their monocles dangling down from their necks. The older one gestured with his hand, inviting Judy to their table.

They became good friends.

Judy has no idea how long Mark had known Pierre before they met her. They shared an interest in outdoor sports: skiing and skating in winter, swimming and hiking in summer.

The following summer, Pierre and Mark invited Judy on a hiking trip near French River in Northern Ontario. They took turns driving, while Judy sat in the back seat like a child. At the campsite, she watched them pitch the tents and light the kerosene stove to make fresh coffee and scrambled eggs for breakfast, pancakes for lunch, and chicken on a bonfire for dinner. The hiking trails they had chosen were treacherously long and difficult. Pierre usually walked silently ahead of the team, sometimes using a compass for directions in the woody areas. He wore a lumberjack flannel shirt of black and red squares; his sandy brown hair looked quite messy with dirt, bits of leaves, cobwebs, and bird droppings. He looked completely different from the man in a French-tailored suit sitting at a European bakery in College Park in downtown Toronto. Mark, on the other hand, wore his usual Toronto outfit in the woods, looking somewhat overdressed, but not awkward. With his hands in his pockets, he followed Pierre closely, as if they were strolling down Yonge Street instead of roughing it in the woods. Judy tried to keep up with the two tall guys, sometimes running behind them and panting a bit in order not to fall behind, but she never asked them to slow down for her.

"We don't mind having you, do we, Mark?" Pierre teased Judy more than once, looking at Mark, who was making pancakes for lunch on the camp stove.

"No, we don't," Mark replied, flipping a pancake in the air.

"Because you are the only woman who can keep up with us," said Pierre proudly, putting down three tinplates for lunch, as if he were giving out an award to the finalist of a physical endurance contest.

Pierre liked to flirt with Judy; had a way with pretty women. Being an engineer, Mark was not as smooth with words. He considered Judy a friend he shared with Pierre, whom he had reminded of the fine line of their friendship.

One summer Pierre went to France for business. Shortly after his departure, Judy asked Mark if he could pick her up from a local hospital. She had been scheduled for a small operation. Mark became anxious; he wanted to ask Judy what kind of operation she would go through, but reticent as he was with women, he didn't know how to address a young Chinese woman about her health.

On the day of the operation, when Mark arrived at the hospital in Pierre's sporty car, Judy was still under anesthesia. Sitting in the waiting room, Mark learned that some women were there for abortions.

Was Judy here for the same operation? If she was, who had got her pregnant in the first place? And this irresponsible man didn't even show up to take her home? Mark couldn't believe a smart and healthy woman like Judy could be so vulnerable after all. Sitting there in the waiting room, a disturbing thought suddenly dawned on him: this irresponsible man could well be his buddy Pierre, who seemed to have taken a serious interest in the girl. If it was Pierre who got Judy pregnant, did he know he had messed up her life before taking off for France by himself?

"Selfish pig!" Mark cursed Pierre, partly to declare his own innocence to the others in the waiting room. "When he comes back, I will teach him a lesson!" he continued his monologue, surprising even himself.

Later when he had cooled off, Mark asked himself whether he was jealous of Pierre. No, he declared, definitely not. But Pierre, his best friend, had no right to violate their unspoken gentlemen's agreement concerning their platonic friendship with the lovely Chinese girl.

Judy was too drugged to notice whether Mark was too embarrassed to hold her arm in the waiting room. She had not heard what Mark uttered in the car, nor realized how much his feelings had been hurt.

In the fall, Pierre came back from Paris loaded with energy and with news to share. Mark and Judy went to the airport to pick him up. In the following weeks, the trio went out for dinner several times. Mark didn't bring up Judy's visit to the hospital, at least not at the dinner table. Judy wondered whether he had mentioned it to Pierre behind her back. She sensed, from Mark's tightlipped manner, that he had already spoken to Pierre about her hospital visit during his absence. Pierre seemed to leave decisions to Mark more often now when they went out together.

Judy seldom saw her friends over the ski season. The two men volunteered as weekend ski patrols in the Blue Mountain area. Occasionally, when the three met for dinner, Judy listened to the men talking animatedly about the various skiing adventures they had encountered.

She wished she could ski as well as them, so that she could join them on the dangerous slopes. But they never mentioned a word about taking her with them, and Judy didn't ask either.

One winter, Judy didn't see Mark and Pierre for the longest time. Near the end of the ski season, she called them and left a greeting in the voice mail. Two weeks later, Pierre called back. "Judy, would you like to join me for coffee at St Michael's Hospital?"

Judy rushed to the trauma hospital on Queen Street. Pierre was waiting for her in the lobby, sitting in a wheelchair. Both his legs, from the knee down to the ankle, were covered in plaster and bandages, and his left arm was in a sling. Tears welled up in Judy's eyes before she could say hello.

"I am much better now, Sweetie, you see, all in one piece," Pierre grinned. "Ouch! Can't move my shoulders yet, but you should have seen me a month ago . . ."

"Where is Mark?" Judy asked anxiously, wiping her tears.

"We are going to see him, in fact, right now,"

Pierre asked her to push him and she took him back through the winding passageways into an elevator.

The door of the ward was ajar; it was so still inside that Judy was reminded of a Chinese saying about hearing a needle drop. She gently pushed the door open. A single hospital bed stood bathed in a filtered, soft warm sunlight in the middle of the room. Inside the tucked-in blankets was a familiar and yet not-so-familiar face of an old man: eyes closed, a feeding tube attached to his throat, his nose covered with an oxygen mask, and a few strands of hair spread limply across his forehead.

Judy shuddered.

Was this Mark, their buddy, lying there so still?

"He has been in a coma since the accident," Pierre explained. "Originally the doctor said he would wake up in a week, then two weeks, but now a whole month has passed, they said he might never wake up again because of his advanced age."

Judy picked up Mark's left hand. She realized, for the first time, that he had extremely large hands. His fingers were stretched out, and there were a few light brown age spots visible on the back of his palms.

"How old is Mark?" she asked, stroking the soft skin.

"Seventy-five," Pierre answered, "not bad eh, at his age to be selected as a ski patrol?"

During the following month, Judy rushed down to St Mike's every afternoon after work. Pierre would be waiting for her in the lobby. She would push Pierre's wheelchair and they would go up. Stationing Pierre on one side of Mark, Judy would go and sit on the other side. The nurses told them to talk to Mark about whatever they thought would interest him. So they had made up a list of topics, from famous skiing resorts in the world to Mark's hometown, Prague, in the Czech Republic, to sports and travel, and almost every day they talked about Mark's favourite Chinese restaurant, the Mandarin Buffet at Yonge and Eglinton.

Pierre promised Judy that after he and Mark recovered, the trio would go to Europe for a long vacation. Judy would write down their plans on the plaster casts of both men until the casts were covered with her handwriting. Two months passed. Judy and Pierre had recycled their topics many times, and yet Mark lay there snuggly inside the sheets, inert. His hands felt warm, his forehead perspired a little sometimes, but he was as motionless as he had been when he was brought in by the ambulance.

Two months after the accident, Pierre was discharged from the hospital and moved to a rehabilitation centre. Judy continued to visit Mark on her own every day after work. She usually started her visit by asking him how he was keeping; she stroked his hands gently and raised and lowered his arms for five minutes. She would ask Mark something specific and pause for him to respond. To keep their conversation flowing, she had to speak in his voice back to herself, sort of impersonating Mark. She didn't know what Mark would say in some situations, and she apologized to him for not being able to understand him completely.

It didn't take long before she had gone through the entire list of topics that she and Pierre had developed together. One day, sitting beside Mark and searching for new subjects, she suddenly realized that they had avoided one subject altogether.

"Mark, I love you." Judy's voice was soft, but trembling. "Mark, Judy loves you. I hope you can hear me. Wake up, Mark, why don't you wake up if you care about me as much as I do about you? Please don't disappoint me, Mark. Try to open your eyes now, Mark, if you can hear me." She whispered in his ear, holding his right hand tightly with both of hers.

Mark's eyelids started to twitch at that moment. He had been in a coma for one hundred and three days. Judy stared. Mark's eyelashes were quivering. Something miraculous was happening. She ran down the corridor to inform the nurses' station.

"Mark is awaking! Mark is awaking!"

The nurses were also amazed. "A miracle! A miracle of friendship!"

Mark opened his eyes slowly. He struggled to move his lips, but no sound came out. Judy stroked his forehead gently and affectionately as if he were her child.

Mark spent the next two years in rehabilitation, learning to speak, to walk, and eventually to skate again. Pierre sold his condo and went back to France for good. The three of them never made it to Europe for a vacation together. After Pierre's departure, Judy and Mark would meet on Wednesday evenings at Marks' favourite Chinese restaurant.

"Hello, Darling," Mark greeted Judy at the entrance to the Mandarin, putting Judy on the spot, making her blush in the presence of the hostess, who was about to lead them to the table.

Judy wondered whether the old man had actually heard what she had said to him in the hospital in order to wake him up from the coma. Did he realize that her conversation was a part of his therapy? And that love was the subject she had thought of only that day? Judy laughed to herself. Maybe she would have to live up to her promise.

At the table, Judy sat on Mark's right, the side of his better ear. "Did you have a chance to listen to the BBC morning news today?" asked Mark.

"No, I didn't, did I miss anything exciting?"

Judy looked at Mark with surprise. This old man, who refuses to follow the media, has in fact never even bought a TV, why is he now suddenly interested in the news?

"Something about a health supplement called HGH. The abbreviation stands for human growth hormone. Do you know anything about it?"

Mark paused, waited for Judy to answer.

Judy raised her eyebrows, a little alarmed.

"I heard HGH can turn back the human biological clock and give youth back to old folks like me! Imagine old men having youthful bodies with muscles and strong bones, and no crooked backs." Mark's eyes shone with a rarely seen excitement.

"That would be incredible!" Judy exclaimed enthusiastically. She started to imagined Mark straightening up his back, and his skinny arm bulging with muscles.

"But the problem is there will be too many old monsters like me walking on this planet for too long." Mark laughed sarcastically. He swallowed a spoonful of hot and sour soup, and bit into a crispy vegetable spring roll. "Personally, I wouldn't mind enjoying Mandarin Buffet for many more years, ha, ha."

"What would come next, Mark, maybe the longevity bills after all?"

Judy remembered the story of an ancient Chinese emperor, who sent five hundred virgins of each sex across the East China Sea in search of longevity grass. "The boys and girls landed on an island, but couldn't find any vegetation that would keep people young forever. So instead of returning to China to have their heads cut off, they decided to settle down on the island, and that is the origin of Japan."

"Aren't the Chinese glad that the virgins didn't find the longevity grass? Otherwise they would still be ruled by the same egomaniac emperor," Mark laughed.

Dinner was proceeding slowly; Mark and Judy went from Chinese stir-fry to roast beef, to sushi, salads, and eventually to fruits and sweets. Mark told Judy that he had originally planned to go back to Prague. "But if the HGH can work a miracle out of my old bones," he said, "I might just stay in Canada to keep you company!"

"Do you have friends back home?"

"Very few now, and each year someone dies," he sighed. "And there was this girl, do you remember the photo I showed you several weeks ago? It was a black and white photo, taken on the balcony of an apartment building in Paris before World War Two. At that time we were students at the University of Paris auditing Madame Curie's lectures. The girl's name was Zora, a very smart and pretty girl. I should have married her, but because of the war, I didn't. Later I found out she had married the other chap. In the seventies, I heard her husband had passed away, so I went back to look for her. Unfortunately, she had developed multiscoliosis. When I went to the hospital to visit her, I didn't know what to do. I said goodbye and left."

"So you don't know what happened to Zora afterwards?" Judy asked.

"No," sighed Mark.

They ate in silence, Mark lost in deep thought. After a while, he said to Judy, "There was a tall boy leaning against the balcony door in the same photo. He would have become a smart physicist, but he was killed by the Nazis just one week before the war ended."

"Do you have any other friends back in Prague?" Judy asked hopefully.

"Yes, there is this other girl. Her name is Olga. She and I are the only survivors from our class. But she is in a wheelchair."

Judy wondered why Mark referred to his university classmates as boys and girls; if living, they would be in their eighties or nineties.

"If there had been HGH at that time, maybe Zora's disease could have been treated," Mark commented softly.

Spring time again. The leaves were turning green overnight. Cherry blossoms were bursting out on hundreds of branches in the park.

Mark was hoping the same miracle would happen to his old body. After carefully reading about HGH, he decided to become a guinea pig. After all, he would be ninety years old this year, and had nearly died once, what did he have to lose? If he took advantage of today's advanced biotechnology, he might be able to extend his precious time on earth. He imagined his old body undergoing a revolutionary makeover and himself changing the routine of his daily life. Instead of strolling down Mount Pleasant Cemetery, reading the tombstones and familiarizing himself with the stages of the last journey, he would buy a computer and start using the Internet. If HGH gave him a new life, he would visit the downtown malls from time to time to pick up some fashionable outfits. He might even be happily surprised by a few reborn desires from his youthful days in Paris. The anticipation of an exciting, brand-new life kept him awake at night in this spring season.

Early summer. Judy met Mark for afternoon coffee and dessert at Sweet Gallery on Mt Pleasant and Eglinton East. The restaurant was famous for its European pastry, and Judy was aware that Prime Minister Jean Chretien had been there for dessert when he was young.

"What do you fancy today, Darling?" Mark asked.

"You know what I like." Judy smiled at Mark and they both went to the display counter. They both liked the apple strudel here. For Mark, it reminded him of his mother's cooking which he said was the best in the world. Judy chose it because it was less sweet.

"I think today we should choose something different, for a change, what do you say, Darling?"

Mark's suggestion surprised Judy.

"I'll have a slice of carrot cake then, my second favourite," answered Judy cheerfully.

Mark had a slice of blueberry pie without topping. "Blueberries are full of antioxidants," he said.

Two years after Mark recovered from the accident, he broke his Achilles tendon in his left foot while jogging on the sidewalk. His doctor didn't attach the broken ends right away, leaving Mark permanently lame.

Nevertheless, nothing could stop him. Right now, the two of them having come out of Sweet Gallery, Mark was climbing up a slope, taking a short cut across a park, instead of walking on the sidewalk down to the intersection. Judy watched the old man from behind, his spine bent and partially revealed under his T-shirt, his body tilted left.

"Darling," Mark stopped outside Davisville station. "Thank you for listening to my old nonsense. I wish I could be younger and share the interests of your generation." He leaned over to give her a kiss as usual. But instead of pecking her on the cheeks, this time he pushed his lips onto hers. Judy was stunned; standing on the sidewalk in the midst of pedestrians, she didn't know what to do except open her mouth and let in his tongue—it tasted like blueberry.

Throughout the year, Judy continued to meet Mark for dinner at the Mandarin on Wednesday evenings. When she couldn't make it, he was reluctant to change the evening and went alone. He reported to Judy any minute changes that his old body was undergoing from his HGH therapy.

"Sometimes I am rather depressed," he once said. "Maybe nothing can really grease these rusty old joints and make me run again. Judy darling, I am afraid," confessed the old man.

Earlier that spring Mark called Judy to inform her that he had bought a one-way ticket for Prague. Judy didn't argue with him, knowing that his decision would be final.

One morning Judy came down to the kitchen for breakfast and noticed the tall cactus lying on top of the African violets.

"My goodness, what has happened?" she screamed. The cactus had crashed onto the blue violets and nearly broken their delicate stems. Judy picked up a roll of newspaper to help her lift up the prickly cactus. Carefully she put the roots back into the pot and patted the loose soil solid.

Since that day, Judy has become anxious. Whenever she is in the kitchen to inspect her plants, she seems to be weighed down by a strange feeling. "Is this an omen? Did something happen to Mark?"

Two weeks after she transplanted the cactus, Judy notices that it has started to lean against the wall as if too tired to stand on its own. A week later, the cactus starts to shrink. All she can do is watch it wither and change its colour daily. Soon it dries up and dies.

One day in the late summer, Judy hits a Czech website, and reads about the writer Karel Capek. Mark had mentioned him to her. On the website is a quotation. Capek says, "Americans seemed more interested in the size of things than in the soul of things." Suddenly Judy thinks she has just started to understand her friend Mark.

The Chinese Knot

HER MEETING WITH JENNIE MCDONALD for coffee in Bloor West Village has brought Luanne Lu back to the streets where she and Steve Jackson used to stroll on Sunday afternoons. Since they broke up three years ago, she hasn't been back, until today. It is early July, and there is a warm breeze; Luanne wears a blue cotton summer dress, hand-dyed in southern China, with yellow and red flowers printed around the crew neck and along the hem of the skirt. She strolls along the sidewalk, her skirt bouncing up and down her legs, her head tilted upward towards the store signs. She loves these traditional family business stores, Dianna's Flower Shop, Alga's European Bakery, Smith's Shoe Store, Lynns' Chinese Boutique; and then Starbucks comes into sight.

"Hello, Jennie!" Luanne waves. Her friend Jennie sits at a small glass table parasoled by a large sun umbrella outside the coffee shop.

"How *are* you?" Jennie stands up, opening her arms to give Luanne a hug; stepping back, she inspects Luanne from head to toe. "I like your dress. It's *so* elegant." She draws out her emphasis. "Did you get it from Lynns' in the Village?"

"No, I bought it last year when I was travelling in China. Now, stand back, let me take a good look at you, Jennie, tight half pants and sleeveless top!" Luanne says admiringly, patting her friend's bare

103

shoulders. "You look absolutely youthful today."

"Really, Lulu?"

The two of them walk to the counter and return with their orders.

"I like your skin tone, Lulu," Jennie says, staring at Luanne. "What brand of foundation did you use today?"

Sipping her tea slowly, Luanne doesn't answer. Makeup? Jennie should know that she never wears makeup except lipstick. She looks at Jennie—dark skin, smooth and shiny, free of freckles or wrinkles; Luanne thinks to herself, you don't need any foundation.

"Steve says hello," Jennie interrupts Luanne's thoughts.

"Oh . . . I didn't think you would tell him about our meeting."

"Why not? He is lonely. He has dated several women, but he said he can never forget you." Jennie gives Luanne a meaningful look.

Luanne remembers a few years back when the four of them went camping in Algonquin Park. "How is Joe?" she asks. Joe McDonald, Jennie's husband, is a lawyer.

"Joe is fine. He is pleased I am taking a writing course right now. I want to write kids' stories, like Madonna. By the way, do you know that someone is ghostwriting for the singer?"

"Yeah? So you and Joe are getting along all right?"

"Yes and no. Joe is *not* the same person I knew twenty-five years ago. He has changed so much that he hasn't said he loves me for years. And I don't want to sleep with a man who doesn't love me, no matter how long we've been married. It's my principle."

Luanne remembers what Steve had once told her after coming back from dinner with Joe. Joe had told Steve that the person he hated the most in the world was his wife. Luanne trembles whenever she thinks about this.

Jennie seems to have noticed Luanne's distraction. She puts a hand on Luanne's arm as if to reassure her. "Just to let you know that our sex life is still quite marvelous."

Luanne looks at Jennie, amazed. "I'm glad," she utters awkwardly. She doesn't know whether she should remind Jennie of the principle she uttered a minute ago.

Jennie points at Luanne's left hand. "What happened to your beautiful sapphire ring?"

"After Steve and I broke up, I stopped wearing his ring. At first, I thought about flushing it down the toilet or throwing it down on the subway tracks."

"Why? It's a beautiful ring."

"So, I didn't throw it away. The ring is in my dresser in the bedroom."

"I always wear my wedding ring even though Joe is not the same Joe." Jennie stretches out her left hand; a diamond ring sparkles under the sun.

"I think wearing a ring is more psychological than a ritual for women," Luanne comments.

"I don't know, but you may be right. Since my wedding day, I have got used to the ring, and don't feel complete without it." Jennie bites into her biscotti; crumbs stick to her lips, then fall. She picks up a serviette and gently presses it on her lips, which are outlined by a lip pencil. "But truly, Lulu, you analyze too much," she mumbles.

The next morning, Luanne gets off the rush-hour bus and crosses Pape Avenue. As she hastens, she thinks she may just make it on time for her nine o'clock ESL class in the community centre.

"Teacher Lu—teacher—Lu, wait, wait for me!"

A man is calling out to her from behind. It must be a student of hers, Luanne thinks. Chinese like to call teachers by their job title.

It is Mr Zhong. Luanne greets him, continuing to walk briskly. Mr Zhong is out of breath, trying to keep up with his teacher. "Teacher Lu, this morning I went to Coffee Time to practice my English. Here, I've got you a coffee," he says enthusiastically, handing Luanne a paper cup.

"You did? You should be proud of yourself. You have ordered your first breakfast in English. How much do I owe you for the coffee?" They are at the front gate of the community centre.

"No thank, no thank," Mr Zhong waves his hand vigorously. Then in Chinese, he asks Luanne, "Would I be able to take a few minutes of your precious time after class?"

"Sure," Luanne laughs. Mr Zhong's polite Chinese reminds her of a way of speech she hasn't heard much since she came to Canada.

Luanne has been teaching ESL to new immigrants for more than a decade. The Canadian government recently opened the door to new immigrants from Mainland China, and since then Mandarin speakers have gradually filled up her morning ESL class. Two weeks ago, Mr Zhong walked into her classroom; dressed in a formal business suit, he looked as if he were there to attend a business convention. Tall and stoutly built with a square face, he had a northern Chinese accent, marked by its clear rising and falling cadence, that sounded wonderful to Luanne's ear, arousing homesickness.

He sat down in the middle of the front row, right under the teacher's eyes. Luanne felt she was being scrutinized as Mr Zhong rolled his eyes under his thick, dark eyebrows. After testing his English, she was even more impressed. The rest of the class became aware of their teacher's delight at finding her best student so far.

Of course, Mr Zhong is no fool. Luanne has cautioned herself against giving too much attention to one student. This morning Mr Zhong wears a navy blue suit, white shirt, a red tie, and his silver cufflinks shimmer under the florescent lights whenever he raises his hand to answer her questions.

At 11:30, class is dismissed. After the other students have departed, Mr Zhong gently closes the doors. He pulls over two chairs to where Luanne is standing.

"So what can I do for you?" Luanne looks at Mr Zhong, hoping he will be quick. She has an afternoon class to teach at another location.

"Sit down, Teacher Lu, please sit down." They sit down face to face, their knees almost touching. "Teacher Lu, I don't know how to talk to you about this. I am embarrassed," Mr Zhong stammers.

Luanne smiles at her bright student, reassuring him that she is listening. "Please tell me what it is. I'll do my best to help you."

"I came to Toronto to attend a conference on a three-month visitor's visa. But I don't want to go back to China, I want to stay in Canada permanently. Now two months have passed, so I am getting anxious. I would like to change my status in Canada before my visa expires." Mr Zhong looks at Luanne with pleading eyes.

"Do you mean you want to apply for immigration?"

Luanne quickly assesses the case; she has seen similar situations many times before.

"Yes, I like Canada very much, I want to stay."

"That's fine. You can apply for immigration by yourself or through a lawyer. If you need a lawyer, I can refer you to a friend of mine, who can advise you professionally. As your ESL teacher, I can write you a reference letter about your level of English." Luanne is relieved that Mr Zhong's request is not beyond her limited power as a contract ESL teacher.

"Thank you, thank you, I sincerely appreciate your suggestion." Mr Zhong picks up both of Luanne's hands and shakes them. "Teacher Lu, to tell you the truth, I have already consulted some immigration lawyers in Chinatown. Some suggested that the fastest and safest way to get landed would be if, if . . ." Mr Zhong pauses in the middle of his sentence.

Waiting for Mr Zhong to complete his sentence, Luanne thinks she should make it clear to him that she has no idea how to speed up the immigration process. From what she has heard, it usually takes about two to three years if applied from within the country.

"OK, OK, let me be straightforward," Mr Zhong interrupts Luanne's train of thought. "If you really, I mean, really want to help me out, would you—would you please—" Mr Zhong stares at his teacher of two weeks for a long minute, and then he drops a bomb. "Would you mind marrying me for a year?"

Luanne can't believe what she's heard. She stands up abruptly, her chair squeaking sharply behind her. Did she hear him wrong, or is this guy crazy? "What did you ask me to do?"

"Please, please don't raise your voice. You don't want others to hear our conversation. I have just asked you nicely if you would marry me for one year." Mr Zhong blushes a little, but his voice is no longer shaky. "You see if I am married to a Canadian, I could get my immigration papers much faster. But let me make it clear to you: this marriage is only a business arrangement. What that means is that we would be husband and wife on paper, but in reality, I promise you I will never bother you. You live your life and I live mine. After a year, we will divorce. After that, I will disappear from your sight forever, and you will never see me again." Mr Zhong pauses for Luanne.

Luanne stands there stiffly, holding the back of the chair; her hands feel sticky. She is shocked by this bold and blunt request from a student, who is a stranger to her. "But this is such a ridiculous request," she utters quietly despite rising indignation. "What makes you think I would help you to cheat the government and ruin my own reputation?"

"For entering this limited partnership with me, I will pay you 30,000 US dollars. I am sure you could use some easy money." Mr Zhong finishes his business proposal.

"Why should I sell my identity?" Luanne is indignant.

"Please don't get angry at such a great business opportunity." Mr Zhong doesn't seem upset at all upon hearing Luanne's initial reaction. "Have you seen the Hollywood movie, *Green Card*?" He calmly switches the topic. "A lot of people have taken tips from the movie and made progress with their immigration. Teacher Lu, just think about it, you could use the 30,000 US dollars to pay up your mortgage faster, or to make a down payment for a new house or a condo if you do not own a home. It's free money for a Canadian identity that otherwise won't bring you a penny."

Mr Zhong's voice echoes in the empty classroom. Luanne hears anxiety, and perhaps determination. His northern interrogative tone also conveys sarcasm. She wonders what happened to this man's polite manners that had impressed her so much in the past two weeks. Mr Zhong continues, "The reason I've chosen you over many other younger Chinese women in Toronto is because you speak good

English and have a professional job. You would be a good business partner to ensure my success."

In a different situation, Luanne would say "Thank you for the compliment." But now in perplexity she looks at the man who is trying to take advantage of her.

Sitting back against the chair, Mr Zhong softens his voice. "I hope you won't misunderstand me. I really have no personal or sexual interest in you, none of that stuff regarding whatever a married couple does. I love my wife in China. We are divorced in order for me to process my immigration to Canada. A year after my marriage to you, you should divorce me before you receive your last installment. Then I will remarry my wife, and start her immigration to Canada." Mr Zhong's eyes shine radiantly.

Luanne feels dizzy; she is too outraged to think clearly. How dare this man insult her this way. He has exploited her identity and privacy, disturbing her quiet life with the temptation of easy money. At the same time, he said she is sexually undesirable for him. What makes Mr Zhong think she would be interested in his illegal conduct in Canada?

Luanne asks, "If you could please tell me, why do you think I would be interested in becoming your partner in this convenient business marriage?"

"Ha ha," Mr Zhong laughs. His voice rings in the empty classroom with a different cadence from before, as he says, "I made a good guess and took a chance. You see, you don't have a wedding ring on your left ring finger." He sneaks a quick glance at Luanne's left hand. "So I thought you must be divorced and still single."

Luanne looks at her bare ring finger, "But I did before, I wore a sapphire ring for eight years before you came to this class. Only in the last few weeks . . ." She halts her outpouring confession. Why should she explain her private life to a stranger who wants to exploit it?

"Teacher Lu, listen to me, you don't have to say yes or no to my offer right now. Go home and think about it, but please let me know your decision before next Monday." Mr Zhong completes the meeting with a formal ending. "Thank you for your time."

Luanne stands there by herself in the empty classroom. She has no idea when Mr Zhong left. Her stomach empty—lunchtime is gone—she picks up her bag, and moves her numb feet towards the door.

On her way to the Pape bus stop, Luanne sees a middle-aged man waving at her from under a small maple on the sidewalk. She squints at the dark shadow. Who is this fellow? Luanne hopes it's not another Mr Zhong.

"Teacher Lu, I have been waiting for you for forty-five minutes." The man steps out of the shade. It's Mr Wang, who sits in the back row of her class with his wife.

This middle-aged couple started coming to her ESL class a month ago, but since then they have missed at least two-thirds of the classes. On the days they do show up, Mrs Wang usually sleeps through the entire morning. Mr Wang sits beside his wife like a smiling Buddha. Luanne has tried various ways to get the Wangs to participate, including asking them questions in Mandarin. But Mrs Wang just gazes at her as if she doesn't understand even her mother tongue. Mr Wang, on the other hand, apologizes with a big smile, saying "sorry, sorry, teacher," in Chinese. Luanne has wondered why this couple wants to attend her class. She certainly would never expect to talk to them outside the classroom.

"Teacher Lu, I have been waiting for you, I know you take the Pape bus." Mr Wang smiles at Luanne furtively. "Teacher Lu, can you write a letter for me and my wife? We need it for welfare."

"What should I say in the letter to the Social Services?"

"You only need to say that we have been attending the ESL classes this month," answers Mr Wang.

"But you have missed most of the classes. You know I take attendance in class every day. I remember you and your wife have only showed up three or four times this month."

"That's right. We come to class on Mondays only. We have to work on the other days. On our day off, we come to school to learn English. But you don't need to say all this to the welfare worker. We need money to pay back our debts in China." Mr Wang says emotionally, "Please help us."

"But I can't lie to the government," Luanne says.

"Teacher Lu, you are Chinese, aren't you?" Mr Wang asks defiantly. "We are Chinese, too. Chinese should help Chinese! You see, Canada is rich, but we are poor. Now that my wife and I have landed in Canada, we want to pay off our debts in China, then we want to bring our children to Canada." Mr Wang's voice is hoarse, his lips are quivering. "Tell me why you can't help us!"

"I wish I could. But I can't help you cheat the government and the taxpayers. You should know that the Chinese in this country pay taxes too." Luanne wants to explain to Mr Wang that besides being Chinese, she is also Canadian. As a Canadian, she is law-abiding.

From afar, a bus is arriving. Luanne says goodbye to Mr Wang and runs towards the bus stop.

It is one of those long and exhausting days. At night, after putting her daughter Alice to bed, Luanne sits on the sofa with a cup of chamomile tea. This is the only time of the day that she can sit by herself to enjoy a moment of peace.

She presses the TV remote. In no time, the flying pizza, the CBC logo, appears on the screen. It's time for *The National*. Here comes Canada's most popular TV anchor, Peter Mansbridge, Luanne's favourite TV broadcaster. Peter announces the headlines: "One hundred and twenty-three Chinese citizens, who tried to sneak into Canada illegally by hiding in an old unmarked cargo ship, were caught in the Vancouver harbour two weeks ago. Today eighty-six of them have been let go after they provided their identities and applied for refugee status. According to their lawyer, most of them have paid 38,000 US dollars to the snakeheads or the ringleaders to have them smuggled into North America."

Luanne pushes a cushion behind her back. She realizes why Mr

Zhong offered to pay $30,000 US dollars for a marriage certificate. With less cost, a safer and happier route, he is being smart in paying a Canadian woman to marry him for a year, instead of paying a snakehead. The Wangs, on the other hand, might be illegal immigrants from an earlier batch. And now both Mr Zhong and the Wangs expect her to help them, only because she is a Chinese like them.

Luanne feels exasperated.

Suddenly the telephone rings across the apartment like a siren. Luanne wakes up on the sofa with a stiff neck. Rubbing her eyes, she glances at the digital clock on the microwave oven: it is 11:40 P.M. So she fell asleep on the sofa and has napped for nearly an hour.

Who would be calling her so late? Canadians don't make social calls this late but wait until the next day. It must be one of her Chinese friends.

"Teacher Lu, it's Joy from your afternoon ESL class." A nervous voice spurts out from the receiver. "I'm sorry to bother you so late."

"Mmm, what's up, Joy?" Luanne mumbles, adding, "You didn't come to school this afternoon."

"I know. I have problems at home. Actually right now my daughter and I have to leave this place, could we come and stay with you tonight?" Joy's voice cracks, she starts to sob.

"Tonight?" Luanne glances at her microwave again. It's almost midnight and she is dead tired. She wants to ask Joy whether it is absolutely necessary for her and her daughter to leave their home tonight, but quickly remembers some horrible stories she has read recently about domestic violence. "Sure, Joy, you can come," she says. "I'll wait for you."

An hour later when Luanne opens her door, most of her neighbours are sound asleep. The lights in the corridor feel cool and bright as Joy and her teenage daughter timidly step out of the elevator. Joy holds her daughter's hand; her other hand clutches tightly onto the straps of her handbag. The girl carries a school knapsack on her back, which pulls her fragile body backwards. Luanne can see dried tear marks on their faces.

It is mid-July; the apartment feels quite warm. But Joy's daughter, Gloria, can't stop shivering when she sits down next to her mother on the sofa.

"Make yourself at home." Luanne puts a plate of chocolate cookies and a pot of fresh chamomile tea before her guests. The girl looks so exhausted that she starts to collapse. Luanne tells Joy to put Gloria to sleep in her bedroom.

The two women sit down on the sofa in the living room. "My husband wants to divorce me." Joy's eyes are red. "He is threatening to move out of the house by the end of the month. From next month on, he will only pay me $500 each month for Gloria's expenses. He won't pay the rent any more. Teacher Lu, how can I pay the rent on my own? It's $850 monthly, and I don't even have a job." Joy rubs her hands anxiously.

Luanne holds Joy's shaky hands. "How long have you been married? Why does he want to divorce you all of a sudden?"

"Gloria is twelve years old, and we have been married for fifteen years. Back in China, we both had good jobs, but I didn't get along with my mother-in-law, especially after my daughter was born, so we decided to immigrate to Canada. But since we landed here five years ago, we have been relying on his single income. I know he is not happy about this. I don't understand why he now says I am too boring for him. He says he deserves a better and more exciting life."

Luanne sighs.

Joy's story is not unheard of.

Luanne thinks about her generation of overseas Chinese students who came to Canada in the early 1980s. At that time nearly all of them were separated from their spouses and children in China. In 1989, after what happened in Tiananmen Square, the Canadian government granted all the mainland Chinese students landed immigrant status. Soon after, the Chinese students started to bring their families to Canada.

Life hasn't been easy for her generation. Luanne and many of her peers have gone through divorce and remarriage in the last decade. Three months after Luanne was reunited with her husband Hui Sheng and daughter Alice at Pearson International Airport, Hui Sheng decided to leave Canada to work illegally at his relatives' Chinese restaurant in New York City, because he believed he would never find a professional job in Canada. A year later, Hui Sheng called from New York, asking Luanne and Alice to go back to China with him. He had saved about ten thousand US dollars. In the late eighties, ten thousand US was a large sum of money for an ordinary Chinese student to bring back to China. There was even a nickname given to people who had accumulated that much wealth —"*Wan-Yuan-Hu*," Ten-Thousand-Dollar-Family.

"With this much money, when we go back," Hui Sheng said proudly to Luanne, "we won't lose face."

Luanne declined her husband's offer.

"In that case, I hope you don't regret your decision!" Hui Sheng warned her of the obligatory divorce following a year's separation.

Sitting on the sofa, the two women talk about their marriages and families. Luanne says sometimes she envies those couples who have survived through thick and thin after their initial reunion in Canada.

"However, after the children grow up," Joy adds, "some couples break up simply because of boredom."

They feel too exhausted to talk any more, but the two women have made plans for tomorrow. In the morning, after taking Gloria to school, Joy will go apply for Legal Aid. Luanne will call her friend Joe McDonald, Jennie's husband, to ask if he could give Joy a free legal consultation.

Joy sleeps beside her daughter in Luanne's bedroom; the hostess curls on the sofa under a blanket for the rest of the night.

Four hours later, when the morning sun shines on the balcony, and vehicles start to move out of the condo's underground garage, Luanne is already up in the kitchen. She puts oats in the rice cooker, switches on the coffeemaker, and starts to prepare a special hot toast topped with melted cheddar cheese and sprinkled with mixed herbs. This is her daughter's favourite breakfast.

Every morning Luanne starts her daily routine like a robot, following a well-practised schedule. At 7:45 she locks up the apartment door, leaving the dishes to soak in the sink while Alice holds the elevator door open for her. This morning they are running five minutes late. They bid goodbye to each other outside the building, and Luanne takes Alice to her elementary school two blocks east. Then she joins the rush hour crowd to enter the Eglinton subway station. It usually takes her an hour to get to her morning ESL session, but today, after Luanne gets off the Pape bus, she has only three minutes left.

There is a figure standing underneath the railway bridge at Gerrard Street and Pape Avenue. Luanne's heart sinks. She prays it's not Mr Zhong, her suitor for a marriage of convenience. Last night, while waiting for Joy and her daughter to arrive, she had browsed through a free community newspaper she had picked up from a Chinese supermarket. In a classified advertisement section under "Employment," she saw, "Business Marriage, Big Rewards." The listing read, "Seeking men and women with Canadian citizenship for business marriages; successful parties will receive generous compensation." There was a local contact number.

So Mr Zhong was not the only Chinese man seeking to fast-track his immigration through a paper marriage. Strangely, her resentment gave way to sympathy for this man and his wife who had decided to sacrifice their marriage for a year in order to immigrate to Canada. What courage! As for herself, she didn't feel too disgusted now to be asked to become his potential business partner, but who could guarantee that a marriage of convenience would not end up with the parties having a serious interest in each other? As Luanne moves briskly forward, she remembers the ending of the Hollywood movie *Green Card;* did it suggest a real relationship along the way?

As Luanne gets closer to the railway bridge, she sees Mr Wang standing stiffly on the sidewalk. He is quite familiar with her daily routine; he has been stalking her for some time. Luanne can't help but fear the consequences.

"Good morning, Teacher Lu!" Mr Wang stretches out his hand. "Have you got the letter for me?"

Luanne is a little shocked that Mr Wang thinks he is entitled to the letter and, therefore, welfare.

"No, not yet. I didn't have time last night because I had to deal with an emergency." Luanne doesn't sound apologetic. What preoccupies her mind at this moment is whether she can arrive at her classroom punctually at nine o'clock.

Mr Wang steps forward aggressively. "So you don't think my case is urgent?"

"I didn't say that, did I?" Luanne has to stop in her tracks to snap back at Mr Wang. She wants to tell him that as an ESL teacher, her job is to teach new immigrants English, and to help them learn something about Canada and Canadian values. Her job description does not include writing letters for potential welfare recipients so they can cheat the government. However, she wouldn't mind writing reference letters for her students as long as they come to school to learn English. She wants to tell him he has put her in a morally difficult spot. But right now she has no time to tell him all this; it would take long for him to understand what being Canadian really means. She shakes her head helplessly, and then with a gesture, she waves at the man to let her pass.

By the time they get to the front door of the community center, Mr Wang starts shouting at Luanne. "Are you using your power to discriminate against us refugees?"

"Excuse me," Luanne, quite shocked this time, turns around. "Now, Mr Wang, where did you learn that trendy political term? I am impressed, truly impressed." She bursts out laughing in spite of her anger. So, if they could learn the new politically correct or incorrect terminology that fast, she thinks, perhaps they should learn some responsibility as future citizens.

"Now listen to me, Mr Wang, I do not have any personal power. The power belongs to Canada, please do not misunderstand me." She knows she can't really blame Mr Wang for trying to take advantage of the welfare system. It is set up in such a way that as soon as the illegal migrants arrive in Canada, they can apply for refugee status. Then they will be referred to the lawyers in their communities, who speak their mother tongues, to develop a convincing story for their hearing. And as soon as they apply for refugee status, they are eligible to apply for welfare. Luanne only became aware of the system after she had taken the ESL job. Now she can see why Canada has been considered a paradise on earth for international human smuggling. As a Canadian, she feels vulnerable and helpless but nonetheless obligated to live up to the country's reputation. Because of this obligation and the generosity that Canada stands for, Luanne says to Mr Wang, "You will get your letter by the end of the morning class."

In the office, Luanne photocopies the monthly class register. She uses a yellow marker to highlight Mr Wang's and Mrs Wang's names and their attendance. She then attaches the photocopy to a standard reference letter printed by the Board of Education for such purposes. She staples the sheets together and folds them up to fit into a size-ten envelope. She knows very well that Mr Wang could easily open the sealed envelope and toss out the attendance sheet. On the standard letterhead, the teacher has only to insert the student's name, the month and the year. There is no space for detail. But if Luanne adds a paragraph by pen, writing down the dates that the Wangs showed up and the dates they missed her classes, she would probably look too intolerant to be a Canadian.

Luanne seals the envelope.

After teaching her afternoon ESL class in the city's west end, Luanne usually stops in Chinatown to pick up some groceries on her way home. There are individual sidewalk vendors on either side of Dundas Street just east of Spadina Avenue. Most of them are new immigrant women who do not speak much English. Luanne likes to buy vegetables from them because of their freshness and price. Soon her school bag is filled up with mushrooms, tomatoes, a cucumber, some bok choy, three bundles of green onions, and some red delicious apples. Luanne remembers that her daughter has asked her to pick up a few barbecue buns for tomorrow's lunch. Not too far from Huron Street on the south side of Dundas is a Chinese bakery named Dragon and Phoenix. The smell of sweet bread arouses Luanne's appetite as she walks in.

Inside the store, people are lining up with trays. Piles of buns are displayed inside the glass counters: barbecue pork, curry beef, chicken, and red bean buns; sausage rolls, almond cookies, coconut and raisin bread, lemon squares, as well as many other items that Luanne can't even name. Most of the goodies are sold at three for a dollar. How could the store survive charging such ridiculous prices? She remembers the bakeries in the Eglinton and Yonge area and in Bloor West Village. The difference in price between them and the Chinatown bakery is like heaven and earth. She piles up her tray with a smile. She can't wait to see the smiles on the faces of Alice and Gloria when she gets home. The cashier fits the buns into a beautiful box with a dragon and phoenix design printed in red.

"Five dollars," the girl hands her the box.

No taxes and no receipt.

No credit card please, cash only.

Luanne walks out of the bakery carrying the pretty box tied with spirals of yellow ribbons. She understands how Chinese immigrants make a living in Chinatown in good times and bad.

Her shopping all done, Luanne hurries towards the Dundas streetcar stop at Beverly Street. Passing International City, a famous Cantonese restaurant, she sees a large red poster in front of the entrance. Cars stop at the curb to drop off men and women dressed up in tuxedos and gowns as if on their way to an opera or ballet. What kind of event is happening here this evening? Luanne steps closer to the entrance. A handwritten notice with fancy black Chinese calligraphy on red paper announces a nuptial ceremony at 6:00 P.M. for a Mr Zhong Guoqiang and a Ms Elizabeth Tsai. A golden character of double happiness appears in the background of the notice.

"Mr Zhong Guoqiang?" Luanne recognizes the name. She recalls the private meeting she had with Mr Zhong two days ago. Is it the same Mr Zhong? Didn't he say he would wait for her answer until next Monday? In fact, she has been thinking about alternative solutions for him. Since she hasn't declined his offer yet, why did he go to someone else? Suddenly Luanne feels her energy sapping; she steps away from the notice board.

A white stretch limo pulls in from the street. A chauffeur in white uniform with white gloves steps out. He walks to the back of the limo to open the door for the passengers. Emerging from the limo is the familiar face of Mr Zhong, dressed in a black tuxedo, white shirt, black bowtie, gold cufflinks, shining black leather shoes, and a single red rose bud stuck in the lapel. Following Mr Zhong is a small, middle-aged woman in a red embroidered Chinese silk *qipao* and black high heels, her hair coiffed, and several long curls hanging down her delicate face. This must be Ms Tsai, Luanne murmurs to herself. Under the dim streetlights, Ms Tsai looks calm and reserved. She holds Mr Zhong's hand and they walk carefully towards the entrance of the restaurant. Looking at her, Luanne can't tell why this good-looking woman would have been so desperate to enter into a business marriage with Mr Zhong. She assumes that Mr Zhong has informed Ms Tsai of his temporarily divorced wife in China, and their child, who are both waiting anxiously to be reunited with him a year from today. Two photographers are busy shooting the wedding photos. Bright tungsten lights on the red carpet make this look like a Hollywood reception. Luanne steps aside while the wedding parade slowly moves towards the double automatic door.

A streetcar comes clanking along. Luanne doesn't know why she is not running off to catch it. Instead, she is standing there as if interested in the wedding parade. Is she waiting to make eye contact with

Mr Zhong? After all, he was her best student the past two weeks, and he not only attended all the classes, but also answered most of her difficult questions. And now, knowing he probably will never return to her ESL class after today, Luanne feels stupid about paying so much attention to him. But this might be her only opportunity to remind Mr Zhong of his deception.

By the time Luanne gets home, Alice and Gloria have gone swimming in the condo pool. The dirty dishes have been cleaned and piled up on the dish rack on the counter.

"How was your day, Joy?" Luanne asks as soon as she opens the door.

"Well spent, Teacher Lu. Thanks to you, I have applied for Legal Aid. I also met your friend Joe McDonald. He talked to me about the separation procedure. He said he would give my husband a call later today." Luanne can see Joy has somewhat regained her control of life; she looks quite a different woman from last night. However, Luanne also knows that her friend hasn't had time to ponder what her life would be like if she does become a single mother with a teenage daughter.

After dinner, the two girls do their homework in the bedroom. Joy and Luanne sit on the sofa, sipping chamomile tea. Suddenly the phone rings. It's Joy's husband, Paul Chen. But before Luanne can pass the phone to Joy, Paul says he actually wants to talk to Luanne.

"I want to thank you for taking care of my wife and daughter," Paul Chen starts. Before Luanne says "You are welcome," Paul snaps at her coldly, "However, if you really want to help my family, since you are my wife's teacher and she trusts you, what you could have done is perhaps advise her to become independent. She should be looking for a job instead of living off me. As an educator, you could also advise my daughter to finish her high school with good grades rather than fool around with her boyfriends, one after another. Unfortunately, all you have done is find them a lawyer to deal with me, as if I am the guilty party. Don't you realize that, like yourself, I am the sole breadwinner of the family! " Paul hangs up the phone angrily without letting Luanne utter a single word.

Luanne is stunned. What did Paul blame her for? She only responded to Joy's call for help. But Paul did make a point in his angry call, she thinks. Maybe he doesn't really want to divorce Joy. Maybe he is frustrated because she hasn't taken the effort to adapt to the Canadian job market; after all they have been in Canada for five years already. Luanne remembers a Chinese saying: "It's difficult for a fair judge to judge family affairs." Without knowing their family history, how can she judge Paul?

Paul Chen comes to Luanne's condo on Sunday morning to pick up his wife and daughter. By then, the mother and daughter have shown signs of homesickness. Luanne understands why her guests are restless. Her own back aches at night and she can no longer fall asleep on the sofa.

"My mother and sister are coming from Shanghai for a visit!" Paul delivers the latest news at the door. "Gloria, Grandma, and Big Aunty are coming to Toronto! What do you want them to bring from Shanghai?" His excitement diffuses their immediate family tension. None of them seems to want to discuss the one-week separation. Luanne is relieved she doesn't have to mediate in their family affairs. At least not right now.

Luanne's life has returned to its normal routine. She can again get to her morning ESL morning class on time. A week after Joy and Gloria returned home, Luanne feels she should call Joe McDonald to thank him for providing free legal consultation for her student. She also wants to let Joe know that the couple has reconciled at the moment because their relatives are coming from China. A reunion with their older folks might put the family relationship back in perspective.

Before calling Joe's office number, Luanne remembers it's always more polite for a woman to call her girlfriend first before talking to the husband. She calls Jennie on her cellular phone.

"Have you finished writing your first kids' book?" Luanne teases.

"Oh, no, Lulu, are you kidding? I haven't even started the project. Now I have to delay it further." Instead of laughing, to Luanne's surprise, Jennie, sounds seriously depressed.

"How is Joe?"

"Are you asking me about Joe? Lulu, you are not going to *believe* this! I said you are *not* going to believe this." Jennie's frenzied tone sounds unfamiliar to Luanne's ear. She can't imagine what could have happened to Joe, and consequently to Jennie; as a lawyer's wife, she never has to worry about making a living.

"Jennie, calm down. Please tell me what happened," Luanne urges.

"I can't talk about it over the phone." Jennie blows her nose loudly. They decide to meet again at Starbucks in Bloor West Village in the afternoon.

Walking down Bloor Street West and passing the familiar family stores, Luanne feels a little sentimental. During the eight years of her engagement to Steve, she had spent many weekends and holidays in this neighbourhood. They used to stroll down the street hand in hand with Steve's old dog, Bronze, a German shepherd, pulling at the leash ahead of them. From the way the neighbours greeted them, Luanne assumed they admired them for being an interracial couple, a new phenomenon in this nearly white neighbourhood. As for Luanne and Steve, they were really looking up to Jennie and Joe, Jamaican and Irish, who put their faith in a mixed racial marriage in the early seventies.

Three weeks ago when Luanne came to the neighbourhood to meet with Jennie for coffee, Jennie was as energetic as a teenager in her short spandex pants and sleeveless T-shirt. Then, the flower shops were selling seedlings in nursery containers, but today flowers are blooming in planters in front of all the stores, and large hanging baskets with dangling green vines and multicolour flowers are suspended on each telephone pole along the street.

In front of the coffee shop, sun umbrellas are spread out above the glass tables, looking like large blossoms. Luanne checks the faces in the shade at each table before she steps inside the café, where cool air greets her to her delight. At a far end table, Jennie stands up, one hand holding a cellular phone to her ear, the other one waving at Luanne.

To Luanne's surprise, Jennie is in a shapeless, loose T-shirt that resembles a pajama top. Luanne remembers that ten years ago fashion designers were pushing the baggy style; at that time Luanne had to put on garments with thick shoulder pads that made her look three sizes bigger. But the current style for women is tightness, showing off the curves.

Luanne and Jennie belong to the generation of late baby boomers, and in their circle of friends Jennie is the fashion critic. Which is why Luanne thinks twice about what to wear before she meets with Jennie. Today she wears a lavender spaghetti-striped T-shirt to match a wrinkled thin cotton skirt she bought recently in Little India on Gerrard Street. Her outfit arouses some attention as she walks into the café.

Jennie finishes her phone call. "I am *so* sorry, Lulu." She gives Luanne an embrace from across the table. "It's my lawyer."

"Your what?"

"Oh, Lulu, I haven't told you about what happened. You can see I am totally distressed." Jennie puts down her cell phone on the table and picks up her cup of iced cappuccino. Sipping a big mouthful of the cold liquid from the straw, she says to Luanne solemnly, "Joe has decided to move out of our family house to an apartment for himself at the end of the month!"

Luanne inhales some cold air, sits back, waits for more details.

"He told me he has been unhappy for a long time because his life is boring and repetitive. He wants to leave this so-called wasteful zone, and find himself again before he can feel happy."

"I see." Luanne is not totally shocked by what eventually had to happen between Joe and Jennie. "Has he told the boys about it?"

"Yes, he told them last night. But you know what, the boys said they could understand him. They said their father has to slay his own dragon before it is too late. What did they mean by that, Lulu? I am the only person in the family who can't follow his logic."

Jennie raises her curvy eyebrows; her big brown eyes seem dulled by the sudden change in her circumstances.

Joe McDonald, a reputable lawyer, Jennie's husband for twenty years, father of their two teenage boys, and a close friend of Luanne and Steve's for more than a decade, has decided to have an adventure by himself to kill his inner dragon, but why can't Jennie see it, Luanne thinks.

"I remember last time you said you two often have good sex." To her own surprise, Luanne has raised a private matter from out of the blue. Realizing what she has just said, she apologizes, "I am sorry, Jennie, you don't have to respond."

"That's OK. We have had good sex, sometimes," Jennie answers as if she doesn't mind. "I thought that would be enough to keep us together for another decade as it has done for the last twenty years. By then, the boys would have grown up. And I could be living on my Canada Pension. But . . ." Jennie covers up her face with her hands to hide her emotions.

Luanne notices the absence of Jennie's diamond ring. The bare left ring finger, narrower below the knuckle, where the diamond ring sat for two decades. "Did Joe say how long he plans to live away from the family?" She feels pain for Jennie.

"He said for only one year at first, then he said maybe two, and by the end of last night, he said he didn't know and couldn't really give a date. I asked him what if it takes the rest of his life to kill this dragon." Jennie twists her fingers with a contemptuous smile.

"And, what did he say?"

"He says then so be it. I think the dragon he wants to kill is me, because, you see, he is acting as if he is divorcing me."

Luanne pulls her chair closer to Jennie to put her arm around her friend's droopy shoulders. "Do you know what he is looking for?" she asks gently.

"I don't know. He says he needs fresh energy to renew his life. But what about me, doesn't he know I have been frustrated all along as well. To tell you the truth, Lulu, sometimes I want to charge out of this gingerbread dollhouse just as much as he does. You know what I mean, Luanne."

Luanne nods. "What does your lawyer say?"

"Oh, my lawyer said Joe's adventure could be mine as well. I found her name in the yellow pages. She has actually given me more than half an hour of free legal advice."

"Sounds like you've found a smart woman lawyer."

Sitting in a subway train going home, and watching other passengers rush on and off the train, Luanne reminisces over the years she shared with Steve. Initially they were attracted to each other by the differences between them. But in the end when they couldn't bridge the differences, they realized they couldn't keep each other happy and had to let go of the relationship. Luanne sighs. Maybe passionate love is only a temporary phenomenon.

"At the age of fifty, one should know one's destined fate," an old Chinese saying comes to mind. Does she know hers? She can answer only vaguely.

At the Spadina subway station a middle-aged blind couple get in. The man is tall, about five feet eight or nine, the woman short, barely five feet. Slung over the man's right shoulder are plastic shopping bags tied together. His right hand holds the shopping bags while his left hand grips a walking stick. The woman holds onto the man's arm for support and direction. From the top of the man's walking stick hangs a large, red Chinese knot with two tassels. The knot has been tied using two red silk strings woven together in a circular pattern in such a mysterious way that there are no loose ends left. Since the Chinese New Year has long passed and it's almost the end of July, Luanne wonders why the blind man still carries a Chinese New Year's symbol.

The train starts to roll out of the station, heading east. The cabin is full and Luanne hears conversations in many different languages and dialects.

The blind man whispers to the woman in English. "Put your head on my shoulder, take a rest. It's going to take fifteen minutes."

"Let me take the shopping bags from you first." The woman stands up to help the man place his load on the floor.

Watching the couple interact, Luanne is compelled to talk to them. "How long have you been together?" she asks boldly.

"We've been married for twenty years," the woman smiles at her husband first and then at Luanne. "We have never left each other for a single day. And we are not bored yet, am I right, darling?"

"Yes, darling," her husband squeezes her hand.

"I am his eyes, and he is my soul." The woman squeezes her husband's hand in return.

So the woman is not blind, after all!

The subway train speeds noisily before it pulls into Broadview station. The woman stands up to help her husband sling the shopping bags over his shoulder.

"It's Broadview," he whispers to her.

"Yes, darling, so we get ready."

The train stops; the doors open with its musical chime. The woman holds onto her blind husband's left arm; a step at a time and side by side, they walk out of the train steadily. His right hand supports the shopping bags over his shoulder; his walking stick in his left hand detects the ground ahead. The other passengers rush out of the train like drones the same way as they boarded earlier.

The doors close and the train starts to move slowly away from the platform before it picks up speed and dashes towards the next station.

Looking ahead through the long dark tunnel, Luanne can still see the scarlet red Chinese knot swinging in front of her eyes.